Rivka's Way

Rivka's Way

TERI KANEFIELD

Front Street / Cricket Books
Chicago

Library of Congress Cataloging-in-Publication Data

Kanefield, Teri.
    Rivka's way / Teri Kanefield.—1st ed.
        p. cm.
    Summary: Unsure about her upcoming marriage and eager to see what
lies beyond the walls of Prague's Jewish quarter in 1778, fifteen-year-old
Rivka Liebermann takes great risks to venture outside, where her many
new experiences include friendship with a Christian boy.
    ISBN 0-8126-2870-5
    1. Jews—Czech Republic—Prauge—Fiction. [1. Jews—Czech
Republic—Prague—Fiction. 2. Segregation—Fiction. 3. Jewish ghettos—
Czech Republic—Prague—Fiction. 4. Prague (Czech Republic)—Fiction.
5. Marriage—Fiction. 6. Czech Republic—Fiction.] I. Title.

PZ7.K1276 Ri 2001
[Fic]—dc21   00-047653

For Joan and Jordan

*   *   *

According to legend,
in the year 1150, at the time of
the Crusades, the Jews of Prague were
permitted to build a protective wall
around their quarter in exchange for
services rendered to the Bohemian king.
The ancient quarter of dark, twisting
streets and overcrowded buildings
was a community unto itself, steeped
in tradition, mystery, and superstition.
For hundreds of years, these walls
protected the Jews from Crusades and
pogroms and allowed them
to live entirely separate lives.

*   *   *

1

The light through the beveled glass window was so weak that Rivka and her mother worked by candlelight, boiling water and peeling potatoes for breakfast. Rivka's three younger brothers were playing in their bedroom, making enough noise for ten children. Rivka's father was at the synagogue for morning services.

Now that Jakob, Rivka's oldest brother, was gone, their home seemed different—quieter, emptier, and sadder. Generally Rivka's mother hummed to herself, or even sang as she worked, but this morning she was quiet, and Rivka knew she was thinking about Jakob, who, just yesterday, had left the Jewish quarter for Poland, where he would study to become a rabbi. Rivka's parents had argued over whether Jakob should go away for his education. "What, tell me, is wrong with our schools here?" Rivka's mother had asked. "Boys come from all over to study with our rabbis."

Rivka's father had settled the argument by saying, "Jakob has already studied with our rabbis. To acquire wisdom, a man must experience something of the world beyond his own home."

Rivka worried that Jakob might never return.

Some young men who left the quarter wrote letters saying that they had decided to remain where they were. Rivka often wondered what became of them. She thought perhaps Jakob, too, would find the outside world so to his liking that he would stay away. The very idea caused the pain in her stomach, which had long troubled her, to become worse.

In Poland Jakob would live in a rented room near the yeshiva with three other students. Here at home he had shared a room with his three younger brothers, so he was used to crowded conditions. Sometimes Rivka thought he would miss home. After all, she and her mother worked hard to make their home comfortable and lovely. Who would do that for the students at the yeshiva?

And here, they lived in comparative luxury. Because of their father's position of respect, they had four rooms all to themselves, the entire upper floor of their building. The plaster walls and woodland green window shutters were freshly painted. A few pieces of real porcelain from Germany were displayed on the oak hutch in the corner. On a wall in her parents' bedroom—modestly out of sight—hung her father's diploma. He was a doctor of medicine, and because of his expertise, he was at times called outside the quarter to serve wealthy and important Gentiles. As a result, they could afford to buy bread already baked from the baker, Sabbath clothing of fine linen, and candles enough even for overcast mornings such as this one.

Rivka's three younger brothers came in, drawn by the buttery smell of potatoes frying. They chased each other under the table. Their mother said, "Markus, make yourself useful. Go downstairs and see if the dairyman has been here yet. Get going now."

"Can I go, too?" asked Ahvram, the youngest.

"Go, too," said their mother.

All three boys stampeded to the outside staircase leading to the street, four floors below. "Careful!" their mother said. Instantly the boys grew still and closed the door quietly behind them. With the boys gone, the only sound in the room was the light crackling of frying potatoes. Rivka and her mother looked at each other, startled by the sudden silence. Rivka smiled.

Her mother said, "Don't you look pretty this morning, Rivka. Oskar Kara will be a lucky man to get my Rivkeleh."

Rivka hugged her mother, then turned away to hide her sudden confusion. She went to the cupboard for the butter dish and then arranged the bowls around the table.

It was said that Rivka, now fifteen years old, was the prettiest girl in the entire Jewish quarter. Sometimes when she looked in the mirror, she saw the beauty others talked of: her chin was small, her eyes large and thickly lashed, her hair a tangle of curls falling down her back with stray tendrils framing her face. Other times she believed she fooled people into thinking she was prettier than she was. She knew how to smile so her eyes sparkled, and she knew how to watch whoever was speaking so she appeared utterly attentive. In short, Rivka knew how to charm the people around her. The result was that everyone loved her, even the girls who were envious of her beauty and her family's social position. Neighbors and family thought she was a perfect child, obedient and sweet-natured. Her only flaw, it seemed, was her frequent stomachaches, which seemed to get worse whenever she thought about such things as her upcoming engagement or Jakob's departure. Both her parents believed she exaggerated when she described the pain.

The boys came back with the cheese and milk, which Rivka placed on the table. Markus tossed a ball, and the two younger boys scrambled after it. One of them hit the leg of the table, causing the dishes to rattle.

"Stop that," their mother said. "Give the ball to Rivka. Now."

The ball, made of crudely stitched cowhide, was small enough for Rivka to hold in one hand. She put it on the top shelf of the cupboard. The boys knew better than to play with a ball inside. Their mother expected Markus, the oldest of the three, to set an example for Ahvram and Nathan, but more often than not he led them into trouble.

The door opened, and Rivka's father came in. He hung his coat and hat on the peg by the door. Rivka's father was calm, even majestic, with his full beard and gold-rimmed spectacles. He had three neat stripes of gray in his beard, which gave him an unusual and distinguished appearance. Rivka was proud of him and felt awed in his presence.

At breakfast Rivka's father told them that Oskar Kara would be joining them for dinner the following evening. This didn't surprise Rivka—lately Oskar had been visiting them often. Until now, though, Jakob had always been there, too. He and Oskar had been in the same class in Hebrew school and enjoyed talking together. But now without Jakob here, Rivka suspected that Oskar's visits would be more awkward.

After breakfast Rivka listened obediently to her mother's list of what they would do that day: in the morning they would mend clothes, and in the afternoon they would preserve apples. But first her mother wanted to go downstairs to visit with their neighbors. Left alone for a few minutes, Rivka went to her room. She closed the heavy brocade curtain that separated her room from the rest of the apartment. Because she was the only girl in a family of five children, she had a room all to herself. The room, which was just long enough for a bed and a trunk, was so narrow that if she reached out both hands, she could touch the facing walls. Instead of a window, she had something better: a small door that opened to a ladder to the roof.

She decided to climb up to her rooftop garden. Her mother used to forbid her to go onto the roof because of the rats and also because she was afraid Rivka would fall. But now that Rivka was older and her garden was up there, the roof had become her place of refuge.

She opened the outside door and climbed the ladder, which was metal and swayed when the wind blew hard. From the rooftop, if she looked to the west, she could see over the walls of the quarter to the larger city. To the east, between two buildings, she could see past the skyline to the hills beyond. The sight reminded Rivka of the enchanting stories set in faraway jungles and magical forests that Jakob used to tell her. As he spun his tales, she imagined herself wandering through forests, picking wildflowers and eating fruit from the trees.

Of course there were no wildflowers or fruit trees in the overcrowded Jewish quarter. Once when Rivka was younger, her father had come home from the larger city of Prague with seven ripe, sweet, and delicious apples—one for everyone in the family. After eating hers to the core, she asked her father if the seeds would grow into apple trees, and he said they would. So she went to the end of their street where the cobblestones came apart, exposing the dirt beneath, and returned with a jar of soil. She planted a seed and watered it. When the seedling came up, Rivka was delighted. What a miracle it was that a tiny black seed could become a green sprout with first two leaves and then two more. Rivka's mother told her she was being absurd—where would they put an apple tree? There wasn't enough room or sunlight anywhere in the Jewish quarter.

"There is sunlight on the roof," Rivka said. "Then we can have apples anytime we want."

"You are either crazy or out of your mind," said her mother. "Apple trees are heavy, and this building is hundreds of years old. The roof will sag and then break, and then where will we live?"

Rivka had already imagined an entire forest growing on the roof. She said, "But the walls are strong. I'll ask Papa."

Rivka's father told her no, she could not have an apple tree on the roof. "The problem," Rivka overheard him telling her mother, "is all those stories Jakob tells her. He fills her head with every kind of nonsense."

Rivka couldn't grow a forest on the roof, so instead she planted a garden there. For days after finishing her chores she hauled jars of soil up to the rooftop. The man who peddled flowers sold her a marigold and showed her how to take the flower apart to find the seeds. Her garden consisted of six round pots in a row with a mat in front where she could sit.

When the marigold seeds sprouted and bloomed, she gave the flowers as gifts to her mother, her grandmother, and the neighbors, keeping one or two each summer for seeds. In this way she won approval for her garden. Rivka's grandmother said it was like her granddaughter, whom she called the Girl of Sunlight, to love the bright yellow marigolds. She also said it was like the sweet and generous Rivka to give her treasures away.

2

That evening Rivka's family was planning to eat with the Brandeis family, who lived on the floor just below. Mrs. Brandeis had invited them so they wouldn't feel Jakob's absence so keenly. Rivka's maternal grandmother, who often ate supper with Rivka's family in the year since her husband had died, would join them as well.

Rivka, standing by the stove where her mother worked, said, "Mama, I can't go. I have to lie down. My stomach is hurting again."

"After you are married you will not be able to get away with all this illness. You will have duties and responsibilities to your husband."

"Yes, I know." Thinking about her upcoming marriage, even though it had not been announced yet and was still months away, made the ache in her stomach worse. She said, "But my stomach does hurt. It does."

Her father was sitting in his high-backed chair leaning forward with his elbows on the kitchen table, studying the pages of a book. He straightened up and said, "Come here, Rivka."

He looked at her disapprovingly, which increased the ache in her stomach. She walked over to him and stood with her hands by her sides. He touched her forehead with the back of his hand. His eyebrows were lowered in a way that meant he didn't believe her illness. Standing this close to him, she smelled the pungent pipe smoke that clung to his clothing and beard.

He touched her stomach with the tips of his fingers, pressing just under her rib cage. "Does it hurt here?" he asked.

"No," she said and pointed lower. "Here."

He looked into her eyes. The deep furrows on his forehead formed wavy lines. "Go lie down until suppertime," he said. "You'll be fine."

"Yes, Papa."

Rivka turned onto her side, facing the wall, listening to the sounds coming from the next room: the clattering of a pan as Rivka's mother took the cake from the oven, the rustling pages of her father's book, and the sounds of her brothers playing a game with sticks on the floor. She heard her mother rummage through the utensils in the jar on the shelf. Rivka felt she should be out there, helping her mother. Lying here with an illness that her parents didn't believe gave her an uneasy feeling of guilt.

She closed her eyes, put a pillow over her head to block out the noises, and thought about Jakob out in the world beyond the quarter. Jakob had been outside several times, most recently when he had gone to the yeshiva in Poland for his entrance examinations. He had come back with stories of grand architecture, charming villages, street musicians, and wide-open fields stretching on forever.

Rivka thought anyone hearing his stories would want to go see for herself. But her friend Chavele, who used to live on the second floor before getting married and moving clear across the quarter, had felt no urge to leave her home and see the world outside. Rivka's mother, too, felt no curiosity. She said she had everything she needed here at home. But Friedl Brandeis, who lived downstairs, shared Rivka's curiosity. Together Friedl and Rivka repeatedly begged Jakob for stories.

Jakob talked about how people out there sometimes taunted him, calling him a Christ-killer and tugging the tzitzis of his prayer shawl and snatching his skullcap. Rivka's mother, hearing this story, had said, "That is why we stay here, where we are safe."

Rivka's mother often talked of the time when angry mobs broke through the gates to rob and beat the Jews. Rivka's mother had been a young child at the time, but she vividly remembered the attack and lived in fear of another such burst of violence. During the attack she had huddled in a cellar with her family as the mob fired muskets into windows and destroyed what they could not steal, mixing salt with flour and pouring barrels of wine into the street. To make matters worse, the Empress, who disliked Jews, then expelled them from Prague, so for an entire winter all the Jews from the quarter were forced to camp three miles beyond the city. Rivka's great-grandmother, along with hundreds of others, died of illness that winter. As a result, Rivka's mother thought of the Jewish quarter as a safe haven, not a prison, and nothing would dissuade her from this view, not even her husband's opinion that the outside was safe enough to send Jakob away for his education.

Two years before, Jewish lacemakers had been permitted to set up a stall in Prague's main marketplace, but their booth was at the far end where the puddles were muddy and deep. People jeered at them more often than they bought their goods. Despite this, Rivka thought perhaps relations between Czechs and Jews weren't as bad now as when her mother had been a girl. Her father often went on business outside the quarter. He had to wear a round yellow patch and special clothing proclaiming him a Jew, and he had to return by curfew when the gates were locked, but he seemed to fear no danger out there.

Rivka thought that if she could just leave the quarter for one day, she'd be happy. She wanted desperately to walk through the streets of Prague and see the marketplaces and bridges and hills for herself. How could she marry Oskar Kara without one such adventure first?

She imagined trying to tell her father how badly she wanted to see the world outside. At first he would say no. Why should she, a fifteen-year-old girl, wish to venture from the safety of her home? But Rivka would smile and cajole and say, "I just want to see it once." Then perhaps he would relent. Her mother would worry the entire time she was away, but at least she would have her adventure.

"Rivka," her mother called. "It's time to get ready. We will leave soon."

"Yes, Mama."

Feeling better, Rivka got up and wound her hair into two heavy plaits, lacing a decorative red ribbon through her braids. She changed into a fresh white blouse she had embroidered in a pattern of green vines and red berries with thread her grandmother had given her, and emerged from her room to find her mother and brothers waiting for her. The rich smell of honey cake made Rivka's mouth water. Her mother, carrying the cake, said, "Rivka, get extra candles. Markus, take that jug of cider."

Rivka's father had already gone down to the first floor, where Rivka's grandmother lived, to help her up the stairs. The day would come, Rivka knew, when her grandmother, like the two aunts she lived with, would be too feeble to climb the stairs. The idea made Rivka sad.

The air outside on the stairs was heavy and damp. The clouds blocked out all the stars. As they descended, the only light came from the Brandeis's window on the floor below. Dubra, hearing them on the stairs, opened the window to give them more light. She poked her head outside and said, "Hello! Welcome!" Then Friedl opened the door to let them in.

Friedl Brandeis was fourteen, her sister Dubra was twelve, and the two youngest children, a boy and a girl, were the same age as Rivka's youngest brothers. Dubra, a pale, dull girl, had the longest hair of any girl Rivka knew. Unbraided, her frizzy brown hair hung to her knees. Once, in the privacy of their own home, Rivka's mother had said, "Poor Dubra. She's long on hair but short on wits."

Friedl's cheeks and eyes were brighter than Dubra's. She and Rivka had not been close until Chavele was married and moved away. At first Rivka missed Chavele and looked forward to the days they visited each other or met at the marketplace. The time she spent with Friedl only made her miss Chavele more. But as time passed and she got used to Chavele being gone, she found more to like about Friedl. Friedl had a streak of impishness and sense of adventure, whereas Chavele, Rivka now realized, was more docile and complacent.

The Brandeis's home was exactly half the size of Rivka's. The ceilings were low, and the only two windows were small. There was much chaos as they all greeted one another. When Mrs. Brandeis expressed sympathy about Jakob being gone, Rivka's mother said, "God gives us burdens and shoulders, too," one of her favorite phrases.

Then Friedl whispered to Rivka, "Come here. I have a secret."

They ducked into the kitchen closet, which Friedl's youngest siblings used as a playroom. It was warm and close in there, and Rivka could feel Friedl's breath when she whispered, "I have something to tell you. My father will take me outside tomorrow. We are going to the market by the Vltava River." Friedl's father, who traded in secondhand goods, often did business with citizens of the larger city.

"Why is it a secret?" asked Rivka.

"If my brother and sisters know, they will want to go, too. I will tell you everything when I come back."

So Friedl would be allowed to go out, just like that.

Rivka and Friedl returned to the main room just as Rivka's father and grandmother entered, making a total of thirteen people in a space no more than ten paces across. The living room was just large enough for an oaken table with four benches. The younger children would eat their supper on a blanket in front of the stove. Rivka's mother so approved of this arrangement that she often threatened to make her younger sons eat on the floor at home as well because there would be fewer spills.

In the corner opposite the stove was a shelf containing a dozen lit candles. All the candles in the metal holders mounted on the walls were lit, too, giving the yellowed walls a warm glow. It was like Mrs. Brandeis to light so many candles in honor of their guests. And it was like Rivka's mother to remember to bring extras.

Rivka went to greet her grandmother. Each time Rivka saw her, she was disturbed by how rapidly she was shrinking. The only thing about Rivka's grandmother that had not changed since Rivka was a young child cradled in her lap was the sound of her voice, which was musical and clear and lovely. Rivka, who always felt oddly relieved when she heard her grandmother talk, hugged her and said, "Grandmama, you sound so good," to which her grandmother responded sharply, "There's nothing wrong with my *voice.*"

Rivka was quiet during supper. She thought about how lucky Friedl was to be able to see the larger city outside the walls. Rivka decided that she would ask her father to take her as well. How could he refuse if Friedl was allowed to go?

Rivka's father talked about an Italian family who were camped just outside Prague, hoping to be admitted to the Jewish quarter. They'd been forced to leave their farming village near Milan after a pogrom against the Jews. They'd been traveling northeast, hoping to find a town that would permit them to settle. If denied entrance here, they intended to travel on to Poland.

Rivka's father said, "We're trying to free up a few rooms here for them. I told them they would be better off going to Poland, but they are fatigued and want to stay. We have already exceeded the number of Jews allowed in the quarter, so we're raising money to persuade the authorities to make an exception."

Rivka understood there were two kinds of laws:

the laws of the quarter, which must be obeyed without question, and the laws of the city beyond, which could be broken if one had the money. She also understood that her father meant what he said—the family would be better off continuing on to Poland, which everyone said was a haven of opportunity. Jews there could move freely without restriction or curfew. They were not confined to their own quarter, and they didn't have to wear the yellow patch proclaiming them a foreign race. This was why Rivka feared Jakob would never come home.

Rivka loved her father best at times like these, when he talked about helping other Jews. Generally his face was somber and his eyes serious, but now he was animated, his voice containing a note of excitement. Rivka was proud of how he derived such pleasure from helping others, whether through his medical expertise or his political influence.

"If we cannot get permission for them to enter," Rivka's father said, "we'll offer help for their journey to Poland."

"Papa," Friedl asked her father, "how far away is Poland? Will Jakob walk the whole way?"

"If any farmers will offer a Jew a ride on their cart, he'll be there in two days," Mr. Brandeis said.

Rivka's grandmother leaned forward. Rivka knew from her deliberate manner that she planned to change the subject from the painful one of Jakob's leaving. She said, "In a few months we will have a wedding to celebrate."

"Yes," said Rivka's mother, brightening at this new topic. "Oskar Kara is coming to dinner tomorrow."

"We will have such a celebration," said Rivka's grandmother.

Rivka looked at her lap. She was aware that Friedl, sitting across the table, was watching her. Rivka didn't know why thinking about Oskar Kara and her betrothal should so often put an ache into her stomach. She could find no fault with him at all. He was a student of medicine and would be a doctor like her father. He was always polite and attentive, and he made it abundantly clear that he was delighted to be marrying into Rivka's family. Rivka's father, after all, was descended from the legendary Rabbi Loew, and her mother was the niece of their chief rabbi.

Rivka knew Friedl envied her, although Friedl was too proud to say so. When Friedl was ten, she had been betrothed to the woodcutter's son, now a woodcutter's apprentice. Although most girls were betrothed at ten, Rivka had not been because her father had rejected the first few offers. He said he was waiting for a man he deemed worthy. The other girls knew that Rivka, with her beauty and family position, would marry better than they. Oskar Kara, indeed, had been declared a prize: he came from a good family with wealthy connections. One of his uncles served in the court of the Empress and was thus permitted to live outside the walls. He often came into the quarter to show off his finery.

It was Dubra, Friedl's younger and sillier sister, who burst out, "How lucky Rivka is!"

Rivka looked over at her father. "Papa," she said suddenly, "will Jakob be safe out there?"

She had brought the subject back to the painful one of Jakob leaving; nonetheless, she caught her mother's nod of approval. It was right for Rivka to modestly change the conversation away from herself. Well-mannered girls did not like to be the center of attention.

"Jakob will be fine," her father said. "Before you know it, we will have a letter from him."

When they had finished eating, Mr. Brandeis led the after-dinner blessing. They sang through seven verses, changing the tune each time. Dubra pushed her chair near her father's and leaned against him. He put his arm around her shoulders, and she rested her head against his chest. Rivka was taken, as always, by the warm, easy intimacy between the Brandeis girls and their father. Her own father was not the kind of man to snuggle against.

Two of the candles on the shelf had burned out. It was time for them to leave. As the benches scraped against the floor, the boys wailed that they wanted to play awhile longer. What Rivka felt just then was a deep sense of comfort. She told herself that whatever was wrong with her, whatever secret restlessness she felt when she thought about the world outside, would soon go away. This was her home, after all. These were the people she loved. If she could see the city just once with her father, then she'd stop think-ing about the world outside. She'd think instead about her coming wedding. She was their Rivkeleh, the Girl of Sunlight, the model of duty and modesty. How could she disappoint her parents with wayward and disobedient wishes?

But that night she dreamed of flying like a bird through the branches of a forest, and she woke up with an intense longing. She lay still for a long time with her eyes closed, imagining the branches of her dream, gnarled and fragrant, set against the wide-open sky.

3

Next morning at breakfast, Rivka said, "Friedl's papa is taking her out of the quarter."

Both her parents looked at her. "Why?" asked her mother.

"Because she wants to go. Papa, I'd like to see what's out there for myself. Would you take me once, please?"

He looked at her over the top of his glasses. The way his eyebrows drew together meant that he didn't like her question.

Rivka's mother, who was somewhat coarser than her husband, said, "If you think you're going anywhere, you can take a stick and knock the idea right out of your head."

Rivka wanted to argue but didn't. A good daughter never disagreed with her parents. Instead she watched her father, who she knew was thinking about her request. In a rare moment like this, when he gave her all his attention, Rivka felt small and frightened. He talked easily to Jakob, taking a close interest in his education and upbringing, but he seldom talked to her that way. He seemed to feel that the raising of daughters was best left to mothers.

He looked down at his plate and then back at Rivka. She supposed it was the pleading expression on her face that intrigued him and made him say, "Tell me why you want to go out there."

"Jakob has gone—," she faltered. "I just want to, Papa. I just want to see."

He turned to Rivka's mother to see how she felt about the matter. Rivka said, "Please, Mama."

Her mother sighed heavily, as if she simply didn't have the energy to argue good sense into her daughter. She said, "Just be a good girl tonight." This was her way of saying yes.

Her father set his cup down and stood up. "Tomorrow," he said, "I have to take some papers to the university. You can come with me."

Rivka wanted to jump up and hug him, but she held still, suddenly afraid to let her parents see how badly she wanted to go. Instead, very quietly, she said, "Thank you, Papa."

He said good-bye and went to his room for his satchel. Rivka cleared the breakfast dishes, her stomach fluttering. Tomorrow she would leave the quarter for the first time.

Rivka and her mother spent the morning baking in preparation for Oskar Kara's visit that evening. Rivka's mother wanted the bread fresh and baked at home. She wanted dessert to be a tart filled with cherries. "I hope the peddler comes today," she said. "And I hope he has cherries." When they heard his call—"Cherry ripe!"—her mother sent her downstairs with a silver coin.

Rivka was down at the street drawing water from

the well, a basket of cherries at her feet, when she saw Friedl and her father leave for the market. Friedl waved, and Rivka waved back. Friedl's round yellow patch was oddly out of place on a girl of fourteen. Instead of feeling envious at Friedl's departure, Rivka looked forward to telling her that she, too, would visit the outside with her father. All morning as she and her mother worked, Rivka listened for the sound of the stairs rattling. She kept thinking that both Friedl and Jakob were outside the quarter and to-morrow she would go, too.

Rivka had finished rolling the pastry crust when she heard sounds on the stairs. She wiped her hands on a towel and ran to the door. Friedl was on the landing just below. Her father was probably going about his regular work in the quarter now. "I'll be back in a moment, Mama," Rivka called.

Friedl was eager to talk of her adventure. She and Rivka sat on the landing between floors and held onto the railing, their feet dangling. Below was a narrow alley with cracked cobblestones.

Friedl sighed heavily, as if worn out from her excursion. "What everyone says is true. We are lucky to have this part of the city to ourselves, and we are lucky to have the walls to protect us. They don't like us, Rivka. You can tell from the way they look at us that they don't. They raise their prices when we come to their stalls."

Rivka remembered her father saying that to acquire wisdom, a person had to experience something of the world beyond his home. "But," she said, "what did you learn?"

Friedl thought this over. "It's different out there. There's more space. The streets are wider. You can stand on the bridge and see the river flowing all the way to the hills. But there are too many strangers, and their faces are unfriendly. I'm glad I'm back." Then, as an afterthought, she added, "Maybe someday I'll ask Papa to take me again."

Friedl looked just the same as she had yesterday: her cheeks had a flush of pink, her eyes were golden brown, like honey. Friedl squirmed a bit; she always had difficulty sitting still. Rivka could see that she hadn't come back any different or wiser.

"Tomorrow my father will take me out," Rivka said. "He has to deliver some papers to the university, and he said I can go."

"So you will see what I mean. It doesn't feel good to be surrounded by strangers who don't like us."

Rivka wondered if she would indeed feel this way.

"Tonight," said Friedl, "Oskar Kara will come to your house for dinner. Maybe the betrothal will become official. Dubra was right. You are lucky."

"No," Rivka said. "You are the lucky one. Really you are." She gave Friedl a quick hug. Chavele often thought Rivka was insincere at moments like these. She suspected that when Rivka smiled, as she now smiled at Friedl, she was simply exercising the grace and charm that brought her so many compliments.

But Rivka meant every word she said to Friedl. Friedl was lucky because, like Chavele, she wasn't cursed with a secret restlessness.

The floor was so clean it sparkled in the sunlight slanting in the window. Rivka's mother complimented Rivka on her work. Their home was lovely and calm, smelling of fresh bread and spices. Oskar Kara, who only saw their home this way, would think their lives were always this orderly and serene.

Rivka's mother braided her daughter's hair and then wrapped the braids into a coil high on her head. She secured the coil with a blue ribbon the color of a clear summer sky. Rivka was unaccustomed to wearing her hair up. She gazed at her reflection in a hand mirror. "I look older," she said.

"You look beautiful." Her mother pulled a few tendrils loose to curl around her face. "Wear your Sabbath blouse with the lace collar."

The sun was setting when the boys returned from Hebrew school. Their mother told them to wear their Sabbath clothes. They must have sensed something in her manner, because they were unusually subdued. "Hurry," she said. "Get washed. Your father and Oskar Kara will soon be here."

When Oskar and her father came in, Rivka stood beside her mother, modestly looking down. Her mother bowed her head graciously as she welcomed them. Then she nudged Rivka, who stepped forward to take Oskar's coat. Rivka smiled her sweetest smile, concentrating on ignoring the pain in her stomach.

"Hello, Rivka," Oskar said.

"Hello," she said to the floor. She caught her father nodding at her approvingly as she turned to hang the coat on the peg by the door.

Rivka was the centerpiece of the occasion. She rarely spoke and took care not to draw attention to herself, but she knew each person in the room was acutely aware of her. Without Jakob to engage Oskar in conversation, there was more silence than usual. Most of the talk was between Oskar and her father. They talked about politics and the Jewish council. From what Rivka gathered, her father had been able to get permission for the Italian family to settle in the quarter. Markus, Nathan, and Ahvram were quiet and well mannered and often looked at Oskar, then at Rivka. She knew they had been envious and excited, as well as sad, about Jakob leaving for his yeshiva. She wondered how they would feel when the time came for her to marry Oskar.

Rivka ate very little. Mostly she helped her mother wait on the table. Rivka, doing as her mother had taught her, kept a constant watch on Oskar so she would be ready to offer more water, or bread, or stew. He seemed shy, as if trying not to look at her too often. At one point Rivka became aware of a tapping sound under the table. Nathan was idly swinging one foot, knocking his heel against the table leg. Rivka's mother motioned to him to hold still.

Then Oskar startled Rivka by addressing her directly. When she dabbed her forehead with a handkerchief, he said, "Are you too warm, Rivka?"

She smiled at him in the way she knew made her eyes sparkle, and said, "I am fine, thank you."

She looked back down and sensed that he continued to watch her. She knew her mother would approve of the attention he was paying her. But Rivka felt acutely self-conscious. She was reminded of the time her younger brothers caught a butterfly and pinned its wings open for everyone to see. Now, with Oskar looking at her, Rivka felt like a butterfly on display.

She was glad when the time came for her and her mother to clear the table. It was better to be up and busy than sitting there awkwardly.

After they all sang the after-dinner blessing, Oskar and Rivka's father stood. Oskar looked at Rivka as if he wanted to say something or ask her a question, but then her father patted his shoulder and said, "Shall we sit in the other room?"

Oskar said, "Yes, of course."

Her father's desk was in a corner of his bedroom, and he used this as his private space during the day. After he and Oskar went into his room and sat together near his desk, Rivka's mother whispered, "Do you see how polite he is? How thoughtful? He will make a good husband. You are a very lucky girl."

Rivka thought this was true. There was simply nothing wrong with Oskar. And after all, Jakob liked him. What could be more reassuring than that? Perhaps she would feel this awkward around anyone to whom she was about to become engaged.

"We will leave the dishes for now and sit over here," Rivka's mother said. She hid the dirty dishes out of sight, then wiped down the table. Underneath the table the boys were playing quietly. Rivka and her mother sat down on an upholstered bench near the fireplace. Rivka's mother handed her a piece of embroidery. She herself would patch her husband's trousers, but she wanted her daughter to be holding something pretty and feminine when Oskar returned to the room.

"He is a handsome man," Rivka's mother whispered.

"Yes, Mama."

Rivka stitched a delicate blue border on the linen. She had to concentrate hard to keep her fingers from trembling and her face relaxed. She sensed that the effort required to keep her expression light and charming was what put the ache into her stomach, but she didn't know how to explain the problem to her mother.

Finally Rivka's father and Oskar came back into the room. Rivka remembered to keep smiling as they made pleasant talk. When Oskar said good-bye, she again had the feeling that he wanted to say something to her, but he seemed helpless, his eyes pleading.

When the door closed and Oskar was gone, everyone in the room relaxed. Rivka's mother closed the iron grate in front of the fireplace and snuffed out the candles. Then her father said, "It is agreed. I will announce the engagement Friday at services."

Her mother said, "Thank God!"

Rivka caught her breath and turned away. She told herself that her own parents had been strangers when they had married. They, too, probably hadn't known what to say to each other. This painful awkwardness was nothing new, nothing special. Her grandmother had felt this way when she'd married. Chavele had felt this way when she had married Josef Kohn. Friedl would feel this way when she married the woodcutter's son. Every girl had to marry the man her father chose, and every girl had to live through the awkwardness of marrying a stranger.

Oskar was everything her mother said he was. He was handsome and polite. What then was the matter with her? Why was God sending her these mysterious stomach pains and this restlessness?

4

Rivka hesitated to bring up the subject of the outing the next morning. She waited all through breakfast, hoping her father would mention it first. He cleaned his plate and refused her mother's offer of a second helping of potatoes. Rivka watched as he set his knife on the table and stood up. Then, to her great relief, he turned to her and said, "At noon I will come for you. I will be seeing patients in the morning and in the afternoon, so I haven't much time. Be ready when I come."

"Yes, Papa," she said.

It was just after noon when Rivka, carefully dressed in a jacket embroidered in the Czech style with a matching cap, walked beside her father, trying to match his stride. A young man sitting in the gatehouse was reading a book in Yiddish. Before the mob attack of her mother's childhood, the guards at the gates to the quarter had been members of the royal militia assigned to protect the area. But when the mob attacked, many of the guards left their posts to join the mob, so now the Jews paid for the privilege of having their own guards at the gates. This guard was pale and thin, with eyes that squinted, probably from reading too much. Rivka doubted he'd be much use in warding off another angry mob.

The guard looked up and nodded at Rivka and her father as they walked past. That was all. Rivka had assumed that he would closely question anyone coming or going. She would have never guessed that passing through the gates would be this easy.

Now they were outside. Rivka felt as if the skies themselves had opened up. The streets were indeed wider, and the buildings, catching more of the sunlight, seemed to sparkle. Rising above them were domes and spires. The stonework and windows were as fine and intricate as lace.

A flock of pigeons fluttered upward to the spires of a building that Rivka knew to be a church because of the cross on top. She wanted to stop and look, but already her father, a few paces ahead, turned back impatiently, and she had to run to catch up.

They turned a corner onto Křižovnická and there was the Vltava River, flowing right through the center of the city. The Stone Bridge, just ahead, was wide enough for a dozen horses to ride across side by side. The bridge was flanked on either end by stone towers and lined with statues. With the river stretching out in both directions and the spires soaring above, Rivka felt as if she had stepped into an imaginary world of her own creation, for surely this couldn't be real. How gloomy and squalid the quarter seemed compared to this. Prague was indeed a golden city.

On the bridge, she felt the statues watching her. "Oh, Papa!" she said.

"Yes, Rivka?"

He sounded distracted. Afraid he wouldn't understand what she was feeling, her excitement ebbed. Perhaps he'd even disapprove of how happy she was to be out here. "Nothing," she said.

Across the bridge, they walked one block, then turned a corner and walked another block. The people did seem to be watching her and her father, but she sensed no hostility. It seemed to Rivka that they were as curious about her as she was about them. Perhaps they couldn't help but notice her and her papa, because their yellow patches were displayed so prominently. One woman who passed them looked startlingly like Rivka's aunt Frumet, with the same thick waist and mousy brown hair.

"Don't stare at people, Rivka," her father said.

So she studied the buildings, the tops of which were grand and imposing and majestic, and at the shops lining the streets with shutters painted bright colors and windows open to display rows of goods. Rivka wished they could stop and look, but she could not imagine her father wanting to idle about in a shop.

"Papa, are Jews allowed in the shops?" she asked.

"Sometimes. It depends."

His tone warned her against questioning him further. They turned into a square so large and stunning she thought all the Jews in the entire quarter could fit there easily. The facades of the buildings formed an unbroken plane set with cornices, arched windows, and delicate detail. Rivka was enchanted. Men in bleached smocks pushed rattling vegetable carts across the cobblestones, and from the distance came the mooing of cattle being marched along by young cowherds.

Her father walked up the steps of a red sandstone building, which she supposed must be the university.

Just inside the entrance, a man sat at a table. Her father took a few papers from his satchel and handed them to the man. They spoke for a few minutes in Czech as Rivka stared down a long marble passageway flanked with doors. As she listened, she noticed that her father's Czech sounded different from this man's, whose way of speaking seemed clipped and severe.

Her father wished the man a good day, and then they were back in the street again, heading toward the bridge. She breathed deeply, feeling as if she had stepped into an artist's drawing. She couldn't make herself believe she had always lived so near such a sparkling and lovely city.

When they reached the middle of the bridge, Rivka asked, "Can we stand here, Papa? For just a minute?"

"For a minute," he answered.

She walked to the side of the bridge and stood next to a statue that loomed darkly overhead. She looked out over the water to the hills beyond and wished she could walk along the road that ran alongside the river. She wanted to leave the city and see for herself the charming cottages and the fields stretching to the horizon that Jakob had talked about, and she wanted to climb the branches of an apple tree.

She sensed her father watching her as she stood there, and she knew she couldn't tell him these things. The soaring feeling inside her that made her want to fling her arms wide was a secret she had to guard carefully.

Her father had said he didn't have much time. She looked once more toward the hills and then turned to join him. She matched his stride, working hard to keep up. He seemed to be walking faster now. To the right they passed an open doorway. From inside came the sound of laughter and music. Rivka wished they could stop and listen, but again her father was ahead and again she had to run a few steps to catch up. She looked around fleetingly one last time before they passed through the gates back into the Jewish quarter. The guard nodded at them as they passed. Perhaps she was only imagining it, but it seemed to Rivka that her father relaxed slightly once they were back inside.

At home, her mother was in the kitchen carving meat. "Nathan's trousers need mending," she said.

"Yes, Mama."

After a moment, her mother said, "So, do you see why we stay here?"

No, Rivka wanted to say. She understood even less than she did before. Nothing bad had happened out there. People had looked at her, but that seemed natural, as she was wearing the special patch. She didn't understand why they couldn't enjoy beautiful outings more often.

Her mother, evidently taking her silence for agreement, said, "People out there don't like Jews."

"Yes, Mama."

Rivka went to get Nathan's trousers. Her father had said acquiring wisdom required experiencing the world beyond one's home, but she hadn't experienced anything today, not really. She was certainly no wiser. If anything, she had more questions than ever. Perhaps, to acquire wisdom, she had to go alone, like Jakob, so she could pause and experience the things outside. Then she would listen for just a little while to the music and the laughter and even go into one of the brightly painted shops.

She imagined marching alone past the guard at the gate, wandering around Prague for a whole day, and then returning. Of course, this was pure fantasy: she would never dare do such a thing. But the very idea of trying was so frightening and exhilarating that she felt dizzy and closed her eyes.

Rivka sat at the table mending Nathan's trousers. She felt her mother watching her, so she tried to pretend that she was content and had no wayward thoughts. She had always been comforted by her mother's uncanny ability to know her mind, but now she didn't like the idea that there was a part of her that she felt she must hide. Once, when Ahvram was four, he had startled everyone by saying, "Mama, I don't want you to know what I'm thinking! Don't look at me now!" Everyone had laughed, and Rivka's mother had explained to him that nobody would know what he was thinking if he didn't tell them. Ahvram had been unconvinced. His mother's powers seemed so magical to him that he believed she could read his mind if she chose. Rivka understood how he felt.

It was early Sunday afternoon, three days after Rivka's outing. While her mother was washing the casements of the window over the kitchen basin, Rivka went into the room her brothers shared. "I will straighten their chest," she called to her mother. As often as twice each week, Rivka removed and refolded all their clothing. Nothing, it seemed, would convince them not to burrow each time they wanted something from the bottom of the chest.

Rivka folded their shirts and trousers. Ever since her outing she had thought more and more about going back into the city. In fact, it was all she *could* think about. If she could go just once, on her own, perhaps she would stop feeling so restless. The easiest way to get past the guard by herself would be dressed as a boy. If the guard saw a girl leaving alone, he would certainly wonder, and that would never do. People outside, too, would wonder about a Jewish girl out by herself. If she really wanted to be safe and avoid being stared at or taunted, she should go as a Gentile. But did she dare? And would it work?

She wondered which of her brothers' garments could be borrowed without being missed. Markus had a pair of trousers, hand-me-downs from a cousin, which he complained were too large. They were pleated in the Czech style. Rivka folded them and set them aside. Markus also had a loose gray shirt. Unlike a traditional Jewish men's shirt with a deep, wide collar, this one had no collar at all. An old pair of Nathan's shoes would work fine.

She waited until her mother went up to the roof to get a bucket and washcloth, and then she hid the clothing in her wicker sewing basket. If anyone saw the garments, it would appear that she intended to mend them.

Going out on a Tuesday or Wednesday was safest because Chavele spent Tuesdays quilting with her cousins and Wednesdays looking after her infant niece. On a Tuesday or Wednesday, Rivka could tell her mother she was spending the day with Chavele without any danger that Chavele would drop by for a visit or that Rivka's mother would run into her in the marketplace. Going on Tuesday would give her two days to plan her adventure and two days to change her mind.

Next morning, Rivka's mother left her at home to bake bread while she went to the market. When her mother was gone, Rivka cut a chunk of cheese and wrapped it in cloth. She hid the cheese, an empty tin cup, and a water flask in her clothes chest. She had a few coins of her own, which she wrapped tightly in a handkerchief so they wouldn't clink. These she put at the bottom of her satchel. She then found a three-cornered hat, a German-style cap, and a short Czech-style jacket, all of which she tucked into her satchel. Finally she took a round yellow patch from her father's desk and sewed it onto an old overcoat of Nathan's. With that done, she sat on her bed for a long time, resting her face in her hands.

All day she wondered if she did indeed have the courage to venture out alone. Later, when she and her mother were washing windows, her mother turned to her and said, "Rivka. What is the matter?"

"Nothing, Mama."

"Don't tell me nothing."

Rivka continued scrubbing. Her mother went on. "Your father doesn't know you like I do. I know what you're thinking about."

Rivka looked at her mother, then pretended to concentrate on scrubbing, too frightened to answer.

"What?" her mother said. "Do you think I don't know my only daughter like I know the back of my hand? I know something's troubling you. I can see it in your eyes. Tell me what it is."

Rivka could just imagine how her mother would react if she told her she was thinking about going outside on her own. She stopped scrubbing and studied her mother's face. She knew every line, each wrinkle fanning from the corners of her mother's eyes, the strands of gray near her temples, the tiny glints of emerald in her brown eyes. The familiar ache came back into her stomach.

"I don't feel well," she said.

"Rivka, what is the matter?" Her mother's voice was sharper now.

Rivka swallowed. "I feel afraid when I think about Oskar Kara." Telling a lie brought tears to her eyes. Her mother looked at her for several long moments, considering. Oddly, it was the tears that seemed to convince her that her daughter was telling the truth. She smiled and said, "Certainly you're scared. Every girl feels like you do. I did. My uncle arranged my match with your father. Your father is an important man, and we have lived well."

"Yes, Mama."

"When you see how kind Oskar Kara will be, your stomach will stop hurting."

Rivka wiped the last smudges from the window. Sometime later she said, "Mama, I want to spend tomorrow with Chavele." Her mother didn't answer, which Rivka took to mean that she had no objection, so she added, "I want to go for breakfast, so I'll leave very early."

That night Rivka lay awake for a long time. She could put off her plan for a few days or a few weeks, but what good would that do? She would simply think about it every day, and her mother would grow more suspicious. No, better to do this thing and be done with it. In the darkness she told herself again that one time was all she wanted, one time to experience for herself whatever was out there. She understood exactly what she was risking in leaving the quarter on her own. If her parents found out, they would be angry and disappointed. If Oskar Kara found out, he might have doubts about marrying so willful and disobedient a girl.

She felt nervous and excited but absolutely certain of each step. She had to go before dawn. If she went after the crowds were about, there was a greater chance of someone seeing through her disguise. She waited until she was sure her parents were asleep, then opened the door to the roof to let in the light from the half moon, now just over the building. She wrote a note to her mother telling her she would be back before suppertime.

Yes, she had planned carefully. But she remembered one of her mother's favorite phrases: We make our plans, and God laughs. What good were careful plans when anything at all could happen? Rivka's mother envisioned a God of irony, a laughing God playing practical jokes on people who took themselves and their plans too seriously. Rivka closed her eyes and prayed as hard as she could: "Dear God, Master of the Universe, keep me safe out there. I only want to see for myself all of what you have created, your beautiful hills and trees." Sometimes she imagined that God, like her parents, could be charmed and cajoled.

5

The stars were still shining when Rivka climbed onto the roof. In the darkness she changed into her brothers' clothes. How odd to wear Nathan's long heavy coat, so baggy in the shoulders, trimmed with velvet and fastened with a wide belt. His shoes, too, were large, but with some cloth in the toe they fit perfectly. Her hair was braided tightly and tucked into her hat. A white neckcloth around her throat completed her disguise.

On hands and knees she crawled to the other side of the roof where the iron staircase led to the street below. A lamp from the neighboring building threw enough yellow light on the staircase so she could watch her feet as she stepped down. She was afraid her parents would hear the creaking and wonder who was out there. What on earth would she say for herself if the door opened and her father, holding his night candle and standing in his dressing gown, discovered her disguised as a boy, tiptoeing to the street below?

But their door remained closed. Maybe her weight on the staircase sounded like the wind. As she passed each floor, she worried someone would open a door and see her. At last she was safely on the ground. She heard the creaking of cart wheels in the next street and supposed it must be the dairyman on his early morning rounds. She walked past the town hall, past the Altneuschul, a synagogue that everyone knew had been built by angels who had brought the stones directly from Jerusalem. She wondered what the synagogue angels, hiding somewhere in the darkness, must think of her, dressed as a boy and secretly leaving her home.

Across the courtyard was the ancient cemetery, lit dimly by an oil lamp that burned all night. Because of limited space, new graves were buried right on top of the old ones with fresh earth brought in from outside the quarter. The earth settled unevenly, making the cemetery a slanting jumble of stone markers. Rivka knew where many of her own ancestors were buried, including Rabbi Loew, whose grave marker was carved with the emblem of a lion. She imagined that her ancestors, like the synagogue angels, were watching her now disapprovingly.

An alley just wide enough for one person led to the wider Kaprova, which led to the main gate. Rivka could see that it was still locked and that the guard was not there yet. She walked back to Široká Street. More people were out now. Afraid someone would recognize her, she walked through a narrow alley twisting behind the buildings on Kaprova. She walked purposefully, as if she knew where she was going.

When she circled back around, the gate was open and a young man, different from the one who was there the day she'd gone outside with her father, sat inside the gatehouse. The newspaper he read was in German. Her heart pounded so hard she felt dizzy, but she willed herself to stand up straight and look directly into his eyes as she walked past. If she looked down and hid behind her lowered lashes, she'd give herself away as a girl.

She expected him to say, "Rivka Liebermann, daughter of Dr. Liebermann, what on earth do you think you're doing?" But he just nodded in her direction.

Then she was outside, on her own. Next she needed to get out of sight of the gates and find a place to change her clothing again. A faint glow showed in the east. Already window shutters were opening and more carts were coming onto the streets. She didn't have much time. She ducked into an alley so small that a horse could not get through. There she crouched in the shadows and took off the long coat with the yellow patch and put on the shorter jacket. In place of the three-cornered hat, she put on the smaller German-style cap. Now maybe people wouldn't think she was Jewish. She rolled up the overcoat and put it in her satchel.

She was now breaking the law. If someone caught her outside without wearing the required Jewish patch, he might simply bring her home or he might put her in jail and demand that the Jewish council pay a large fine to free her. Being put in jail or brought home in disgrace by the Czech authorities wasn't exactly what she'd had in mind when she'd set out on this adventure. She had better take care.

This time she stopped to read the inscriptions at the bases of the statues on the Stone Bridge. She learned from the inscriptions that these statues were depictions of saints. As she understood the utterly foreign ideas of Catholicism, people worshipped these statues instead of God. Jakob had once told her that altars to the saints were even built inside Catholic houses of worship.

The statues were large and menacing. One, near the center of the bridge, depicted a figure with a tail and cloven feet licking the wounds of an unusually tall man. The inscription told her the tall man was Jesus Christ. She looked more closely at his face. So this was the man the Christians believed to be divine. Her father had told her Jesus Christ was a devout Jewish man, a prophet whose followers later claimed he was the son of God. Rivka's response at the time had been, "But we are *all* the sons and daughters of God." Because Jesus had been Jewish, this must have been what he meant. How odd that his followers had taken this claim so literally.

Just standing alone in the pale light of early morning so near these statues scared her. She had been taught that depicting the divine in stone was impossible, for the divine was not knowable in this way, and worshipping images made of stone or wood was forbidden. But what about just standing here looking? She decided not to risk it and walked the rest of the way across the bridge without inspecting any more statues.

Here she was, doing what was unheard of: a fifteen-year-old Jewish girl going outside the quarter on her own. Maybe this wasn't real. Maybe she was dreaming or had swallowed a magical potion that brought visions. She felt she had stepped into someone else's body instead of borrowed clothing.

She found a grassy place to sit on the riverbank, spread out her coat, and took out her cheese and bread. After eating some breakfast and wrapping the remainder for later, she returned to a square where people were gathered in an open market. Buyers haggled over prices, and hounds sniffed underfoot. It was like the commotion in the Jewish markets, except for the wide-open space. The Czech girls wore jackets and headbands embroidered with brightly colored flowers and birds. One girl, wearing a square cap and a necklace of coral, carried a basket of eggs on her arm.

Rivka imagined that people could see through her disguise. She thought they must be laughing to themselves, thinking, Look at that Jewish girl dressed like a Christian boy. Just who does she think she is fooling?

Then one of the girls approached her and said, "Buy some of my eggs, sir?"

Sir. Rivka managed to shake her head no, embarrassed. She remembered to look directly at the girl, who looked down demurely.

So her disguise worked. People did think she was a boy and that she belonged here. Imagine that.

Rivka had thought that now, in this moment of danger, when anything at all could go wrong, her stomach might hurt as never before. But what she felt was exhilaration. Her heart pounded, and her breathing was deeper. Never had she felt better. Even the air here, which seemed freer and lighter, smelled different from the air in the Jewish quarter. Maybe this was indeed all she needed. She could get her fill of this open market with the breeze on her cheek, and the wide-open spaces, and then, in a few hours, return home content with having had such an incredible adventure.

Rivka was afraid she might be seen by someone she knew from the quarter. She did not want to be brought home in shame, like a child, so she thought it best to leave the city and walk through the hills and fields. She remembered the road that ran alongside the Vltava River and led away from the city. She decided to find it and follow it for a while.

Even at this hour, the road was crowded. She imagined Jakob walking along a road such as this one toward Poland, hoping a farmer would stop to offer him a ride. She wondered if she would ever dare tell him that she, too, had left on her own. She could easily imagine how her parents would react, but Jakob's response was harder to predict. He wasn't the type to get angry. Instead, he'd probably talk to her about how foolish she'd been.

She saw workers, dozens of them, walking away from the city. She approached a man coming toward her pushing a wooden cart and asked him where they were going.

He said they were going to harvest potatoes, what else? Then he said, "Where are you from? I don't know your way of talking."

She remembered how different her father's Czech had sounded from that of the man at the university. She'd grown up speaking Yiddish, German, and Czech with what she thought was native fluency. Now she realized that her way of speaking set her apart. "I'm from Zurich," she replied, naming the farthest German-speaking city she could think of.

This satisfied the man, who said, "A Swiss lad, eh?"

At that moment she forgot herself and flashed her brightest smile, the one that instantly warmed strangers to her. The man seemed startled and looked at her more closely. She turned away abruptly and marched off behind the workers, suddenly terrified. She must remember she was not a girl. Boys did not depend on their smiles to get along in the world.

The river smelled damp and mossy, and the ground underfoot was soft. To her left was a stunning panorama of hills. Being on the rooftop near her pots of marigolds was nothing compared to this. Like Moses, she could say, "I have been a stranger in a strange land." Had Moses felt this frightened yet deeply alive?

At last they came to a broad expanse of potato fields. The workers picked up sacks and digging forks from a pile and walked among the rows. There were girls among them, digging up potatoes, too. Rivka thought she would be able to do the digging. What better way to see how others lived than to join their work?

Should she just pick up a sack and digging fork and begin? She wasn't sure. She wondered what the workers would do if they discovered she was Jewish. Would they jeer at her? Or hurt her? Perhaps her adventure was simply too foolish and dangerous. She wanted to think of a prayer but was too conscious of where she was and who was around her.

A man in a muslin shirt seemed to be supervising the workers. He saw her but looked past her to the others, as if she belonged there. This gave her the confidence to approach him. Up close she could see he was a gruff-looking fellow with a straggly beard.

"I would like some work, sir," she said.

"What's your name?" he asked.

"Sebastian Gunther."

"Where are you from?"

Deciding that Zurich sounded too far away and exotic, she said, "Saxony."

He looked curious. "Where in Saxony?"

"Near Dresden." She had often studied the atlas her father kept on his desk, but the names of the towns hadn't seemed real somehow. She was startled to see that this man actually believed she had come from Dresden.

"Pay is one zlatka per bag," he said, offering her a sack and a spade.

Rivka took them and moved off by herself. Digging potatoes was hard, but she felt invigorated.

Here she was in the open sunshine, breathing the fresh air. She doubted, though, that she'd be any wiser at the end of the day. Tired, perhaps, because already she felt an ache in her forearms, and dirty. But she was certainly having the adventure she wanted. She looked up at the hills as she worked. Yes, she'd remember this forever.

After an hour or two she felt she'd had enough of this. What she really wanted was to walk through the hills and see the forest. Now she wished she hadn't joined the workers because she didn't think she could leave without drawing attention to herself. Of course, if they continued too late into the day, she'd have to risk being conspicuous by leaving early so she could return home on time.

When the sun was high in the sky, some women dug three fire pits at the edge of the field near the river. Soon they were stirring large metal vats, which Rivka guessed must be the noontime meal. Then one of the women rang a bell, and the workers lined up, holding cups or bowls. Rivka took the tin cup from her satchel and stood in line with the others.

In line she noticed a young man watching her. He had hair as yellow as the sun-dried wheat in the fields across the river. With his hair and blue eyes and pale, translucent skin, he seemed more like a colorful drawing than a real person, but his shirt was tattered and untucked. His eyes held a bright curiosity that made her uneasy. Rivka turned away and tried to ignore him.

One of the women filled her cup with potatoes in a heavy sauce. Floating in the stew were bits of red meat. This was forbidden food that she couldn't eat, even though her stomach growled angrily. She still had the remaining bread and cheese she had taken from home, so at least she wouldn't go hungry. She sat off by herself away from the others, and when she was sure nobody was watching, she secretly fed the stew to the hounds sniffing around for scraps.

The yellow-haired man came to sit near her. Instantly she stood up and moved to the thickest part of the crowd of workers. Sitting in their midst, listening to their laughter, she could ignore the man, who again moved near her. What was he doing? she wondered. Did he see through her disguise? Was he going to denounce her as an impostor?

Soon the meal was over, and the workers returned to their rows of potatoes. Again Rivka considered leaving but decided it would draw too much attention. As the afternoon wore on, she grew too tired to enjoy her adventure any longer. When she stretched, she saw that the young man was harvesting directly behind her.

Now she was becoming frightened. Without turning back, she dragged her sack behind her and moved a few rows over. When she dared look his direction again, she noticed he had moved into her row once more. He smiled at her, his face open and friendly. He evidently meant her no harm. If he wanted to denounce her, he could have done so already. She turned away modestly, acutely conscious of being stared at by this stranger.

She had filled two bags of potatoes. Each time she turned in a bag, she was given a polished oak chip to be redeemed later for a coin. By midafternoon, she felt herself slowing down considerably. She was used to hard work—her daily chores at home included lugging jugs of water up four flights of stairs—but nothing she had done had ever been this relentless. The young man came up behind her and poured some of his potatoes into her sack.

"You don't have to do that—"

"Please, Sebastian, or whatever you say your name is. Now, stay quiet or the others will wonder what's happening."

She continued digging into the late afternoon. Soon it would be time for her to go home. She'd slip through the gates, wearily climb the stairs to her home, change back into her own clothing on the roof, and pray that nobody would see her.

Maybe she would tell Friedl what she had done. Friedl would ask, "What did you do out there all day?" Rivka would have to admit, "I harvested potatoes." Naturally Friedl would ask why on earth she had wanted to harvest potatoes. Was harvesting potatoes so enchanting that she had risked getting caught and shaming her family? It was absurd. How would Rivka explain what had driven her?

She stopped and gazed south toward the hills. She hadn't really seen the hills yet, nor had she walked through the forest and looked up at the branches against the sky. She wasn't ready to go home, but the sun was low in the sky, and she'd need to leave soon to be back in time to set the table for supper.

Rivka had slowed down so much because of the strain on her back that she was afraid of the humiliation she'd face if someone noticed how little she had done. What if they figured out she wasn't a boy from Saxony after all?

When the bell rang for quitting time, the young man came up behind her and put enough potatoes in her bag to fill it to the top. "Shh," he said when she started to protest. "I have plenty. I've turned in three bags since lunch."

"Thank you," she replied. She dragged her full bag behind her, and he hoisted his over his shoulder as they approached the wagons loaded with potatoes.

Rivka and the kind young man lined up behind the other workers to get their wages. The man in the muslin shirt held a sack of coins. When it was Rivka's turn, she handed him three oak chips, and he handed her four coins. She was only supposed to get three, but she was afraid to say anything that might attract attention to herself.

She turned away, feeling as guilty as if she had stolen the extra coin. No, she couldn't take money that didn't belong to her. She turned back and said, "Sir, you gave me too many." She handed a coin back to him. When he simply stared, she said, "I gave you three chips, not four."

First he blinked and looked down at his bag, as if he couldn't have made such a mistake. Recovering, he said, "What do we have here? A saint from Saxony?"

Rivka felt her cheeks burning. Boys didn't blush, but here she was, feeling the heat rise from her throat to her ears. He took the coin from her and dropped it into his sack. She heard the other workers around her laughing. One person said, "Who is that boy, anyway?"

At that the young man stepped forward and said, "Come on, Sebastian, we'd better get going."

His authoritative tone quieted the others, and Rivka was immediately grateful. He put his arm over her shoulder in a brotherly manner, as if they were familiar comrades. She turned and walked away beside him. A hound trotted at their heels.

As soon as she could do so without seeming rude, Rivka pulled away from him.

"Are you going to thank me?" he asked.

"Yes, of course. Thank you."

They reached the river and stopped. "Uh, Sebastian," the young man said. Rivka turned to him. Up close she could see he was younger than she had supposed—no more than sixteen or seventeen.

He said, "I know you are not from Saxony. And I know you are not a boy."

She swallowed, feeling trembly and weak. "What makes you think that?"

"My father was from Saxony, and your accent is different."

Rivka felt like a perfect fool.

He said, "Are you coming back for the harvesting tomorrow?"

"No. I have to go now. Good-bye." She turned and walked briskly toward town. The young man caught up with her and said, "Where are you going?"

"Home." And then, "I have to go now. Please."

"All right, Sebastian, or whatever your name is. Good-bye."

He stopped and let her walk on ahead. Once, she turned and looked back. He was standing where she had left him, watching her.

6

Rivka marched through the thoroughfare toward home. Pants, she decided, were much easier to wear than skirts. She moved more freely in these clothes and didn't have to worry about how she looked or whether her slender waist was shown to its best advantage. It didn't even matter whether people thought she was pretty.

She must have taken a wrong turn because she found herself on a street that she didn't recognize. No matter. She knew she was walking in the right direction. She stopped at the sight of a magnificent domed structure with pillars and a glittering entrance. A dozen carriages were lined up in front. Inside she could see a group of ladies and gentlemen, the ladies with their hair piled high on their heads, the gentlemen wearing black suits and white shirts.

She turned into a crooked street and paused for just a moment to peek into a shopwindow filled with glassware. The street was particularly charming, with window boxes and shops trimmed in green. Suddenly she found her way barred by a wall of heavy limestone. The tops of the buildings on the other side were dark and decrepit. Rivka felt as shocked as if she had discovered the walls of the

Jewish quarter for the first time. So this was how her home appeared from the outside: a squalid city within the larger one. The wall was like a hideous slash through a beautiful painting, destroying the charm and warmth of the shop-lined alley.

Abruptly she turned and headed back to the main thoroughfare, which took her to the main gates of the quarter. Just before reaching the gate, she ducked into an alley, and, squatting behind an oak barrel, hurriedly changed into the Jewish coat with the patch. She prayed nobody was watching from the windows above and wondering what she was doing. If someone was watching, with luck she'd be safely inside before anyone could stop her. As she passed the guard at the gate, she gave him a small wave, concentrating on looking relaxed and natural and fearless. Only after she was back inside did she realize how hard her heart was pounding.

She ran the rest of the way home. When she reached the steps of her building, she had to catch her breath for the four-story climb. The building looked no different, as if she hadn't been gone at all. The walls were still dirty white with water spots, the stairs appearing as fragile as a child's toy.

Now came the greatest danger. Everyone in this building knew her, and anyone looking closely would see through her disguise. She was accustomed to running lightly up these steps in her soft leather-soled shoes. She couldn't tiptoe as she had on her way down. That would be too conspicuous now. Walking naturally in Nathan's clunky old shoes caused the stairs to shake as if she were much larger and heavier. She reached the last set of rickety stairs to the roof. There she changed into her own clothing, shaking her head to let her braids fall down her back. She folded her brothers' clothing and put it near the ladder leading to her bedroom.

Then she climbed back down the stairs to the door of her home. She put her hand on the metal knob and listened, as if she expected to hear what her family was doing inside. Pushing open the door, she stepped in. She was greeted by the spicy smell of a vegetable stew that her mother was stirring in a large vat on the stove.

"Rivka, you're late," she said without turning around. "Hurry up and get the bread from the oven."

Rivka looked down and noticed how thoroughly dusty her arms were. Her face, too, must be smeared. She was far too dirty to wash in the basin in her room. "I'll be right back, Mama," she called and turned to the door.

"Rivka?"

"I'm going to wash," she said, and was outside before her mother had a chance to respond. Down at the well she scrubbed her face and hands and arms, and then, trying to calm her racing heart, climbed back upstairs again. Once inside, she said as lightly as she could manage, "I wanted to wash."

"How is Chavele?" her mother asked as Rivka went to take the bread from the oven.

"Fine, Mama." Rivka's voice felt tight. Was it her imagination, or was her mother looking at her too closely?

"What did you do all day?"

"Worked, mostly." This much, at least, was true. Rivka took down the plates and utensils from the cupboard and set the table, concentrating on making it as attractive as possible. Now that she was safely home, she was stunned by the audacity of what she had done. Was it possible that she, Rivka Liebermann, had dared sneak out of the quarter dressed as a boy? And was it possible that her mother would not know?

"I'll get some flowers, Mama," she said. She liked using her marigolds to decorate the table, and this would give her another chance to get away from her mother for a moment so she could collect herself. When she reached the rooftop, she tested the dampness of the soil and found that the flowers needed no water. She picked three of the fullest blooms and took the flowers and the bundle of clothes down the ladder into her room. She shoved the clothing into her wooden chest. Then she took a blue hair ribbon and tied the flowers together. These she put into a small clay vase.

"Very pretty, thank you," her mother said as Rivka returned to the main room and put the vase on the table.

Again Rivka wondered if her mother noticed anything different about her. Her fingers trembled as she adjusted the bow around the flowers. She thought she must look changed after such an adventure. Would her mother see something in her expression to give away her secret?

After dinner, as her father read a book, Rivka sat with her mother, mending clothing. Her mother startled her by suddenly taking her hand and lifting her forearm to look at her elbow. There was a trace of dirt from digging. Rivka brushed it off as if embarrassed to be dirty and then concentrated on her needle. Her mother said nothing, but Rivka feared this was because her father was in the room.

The fire had died down and the embers were glowing when Rivka announced that she was tired and would go to bed. She escaped into the darkness of her room, where she slipped into her nightgown and into bed. When her head sank onto the pillow, she felt sheer physical exhaustion from the long hours of work. Muscles she didn't know she possessed ached.

She closed her eyes and remembered the majestic spires set against the sky, the wide-open thoroughfares, the smell of the river, and the bustle of the market-place. How strange to think that she had always been so close to such wonders—a stone's throw, really—but might have lived her entire life without seeing the larger city for herself. The pity was that she had ventured out but had not experienced what she most wanted to see, the hills and forest. Instead, she had wasted her precious afternoon harvesting potatoes.

Now she had so intense a longing to see the forest that she felt a jitter deep in her stomach. Dare she go again? Passing through the gate had gone smoothly enough. Perhaps she could just go for a few hours in the afternoon.

She thought about the young man who had been so kind. Remembering the blue of his eyes and the yellow of his hair, he didn't seem real. She understood now how lucky she had been. Perhaps if she went again, she wouldn't be so lucky. Had someone less kind seen through her disguise, he could have exposed her, and she would have been brought home by the authorities in shame or put in jail. The angels must have been watching over her and protecting her from danger.

7

The following day, Rivka's mother was drying the last of the dishes from their midday meal, and Rivka was stacking the plates on the top cupboard shelf. Her mother said, "Your aunt Frumet came by early this morning. Her son is sick again. We're going to visit and help out."

Rivka reached up to put the last plate on the stack. "Mama, may I stay at home? I have sewing to finish."

Her mother looked at her for a long moment, then said, "Fine, stay home." So maybe she didn't suspect after all.

After her mother left, Rivka sat in her room for several minutes wondering if she dared leave again. Why was she flirting with danger this way? Was the lure of the forest worth getting caught and upsetting her parents?

Her success the day before had given her confidence, perhaps too much. Here she was, considering going out in broad daylight. What could be more foolhardy? She should feel grateful her adventure had been a success and stop now. Instead she wanted to take another chance. What was wrong with her? How had the sensible and obedient Rivka suddenly grown so foolish?

She changed back into her brothers' clothes, hid her hair under the three-cornered hat, and put a few coins deep in her satchel. She then descended the stairs to the alley below and, keeping her head bowed and her hat pulled low, walked purposefully toward the gate. Getting through was so easy that she wondered why more girls didn't do this. Well, how did she know they didn't? Suppose dozens of girls did this each day, and nobody ever suspected? She imagined an army of Jewish girls dressed as Czech boys marching through the marketplaces and thoroughfares of Prague. The idea almost made her laugh.

Once outside, she found an alley and changed from the hat to the German-style cap. She removed her Jewish-style overcoat, rolling it up tightly so it would fit into her satchel, and put on the shorter jacket. She marched out of the alley with all the confidence of a boy. She crossed the Stone Bridge without stopping to look at the statues and then followed the river away from the city.

She came to the potato fields where she had worked the day before. This time she walked by without looking. If the young man was there, she hoped he wouldn't see her. He had been nice enough, but he could expose her as an impostor, and she felt uneasy remembering how intently he had watched her.

When she was out of sight of the workers, she found a trail leading away from the river and up into the hills. The shadows in the forest deepened as she walked among the trees, the leaves and twigs crunching underfoot. The heavy foliage above her and the seemingly infinite variety of shrubs and plants made her feel that she had indeed entered a magical forest from one of Jakob's stories. She felt like a fairy-tale character in search of adventure.

She came upon a rock with a flat surface like a chair. She piled up leaves and covered them with the long coat. She lay back and stared into the branches. Her braids fell out from under her hat, and she let them dangle.

She was utterly alone, for perhaps the first time in her life. Now that she was this far from the quarter, she wondered if the synagogue angels could find her. What would happen, she thought, if she needed their protection? She imagined the angels flying over Prague in search of her and, like birds, perching in the branches overhead to keep watch over her.

How still the forest was. Occasionally a light wind moved the highest leaves. She looked upward and, seeing apples on the branches, sat up. She had been sitting under an apple tree. Even when she stood up on the rock, the apples were too high to reach. She took off her jacket and hoisted herself onto the lowest branch, which was gnarled and bulbous. She pulled herself up and scooted out far enough to pick two apples.

Climbing down, she stepped first to the rock, then to the ground. The moss was soft underfoot. The roots of the apple tree, large and twisted, came out of the ground and wound back in, reminding her of a picture of a serpent in one of her father's books. She could now see the absurdity of her idea of growing trees on the roof. She sat back on the flat rock and ate one of the apples. The other she put into her satchel.

In a sunny glade not far away was a bed of clover sown thickly with buttercups. She knelt to inspect one of the blossoms and found the petals feathery and light to the touch. The sweet smell of earth mixed with the scent of ripening apples and the musky smell of wood and bark. The slanting light through the trees and the abundance of life all around her made her feel that she was very close to God.

Once when Rivka was about ten and feeling rebellious, she told her brother Jakob that she didn't believe in God. She would never have dared say such a thing to her father. Jakob had looked at her solemnly and, in the voice she imagined he would use often when he became a rabbi, said, "What do you believe in? When you find something you believe in, something beautiful and mysterious that you don't understand, that's where you will find God."

Wanting to find God, she had looked for something beautiful and mysterious that she didn't understand. What she found were her seeds that became flowers. She told this to Jakob, who said, "Yes, God is what makes a seed become a flower." If this were true, then God was here, in the forest, far more than in the crowded quarter. She thought that venturing from home and risking the wrath of her parents had certainly been worth this moment amid God's quiet and majestic beauty.

From the distance came the sound of crunching leaves and snapping twigs. Her first thought, remembering Jakob's fairy stories, was that a wild animal was approaching. She looked for a place to hide but felt as exposed as if she stood alone at the railing of the Stone Bridge.

She saw the white of his shirt and yellow of his hair before she recognized the young man from the day before. Quickly she tucked her braids back into her hat and smoothed her clothes, brushing off the leaves and twigs.

"Hello there," he said.

She swallowed. "Hello." To her own ears, her voice sounded shaky and small.

He said, "I saw you walk by and wondered what you were doing."

She looked at the tips of her shoes. A woodland bug was crawling over the toe.

"But I guess you won't tell me," he said.

She shook her head.

"All right. Even if you won't talk to me, I'll keep your secret that you're not a boy from Saxony named Sebastian Gunther."

"I just wanted to see the forest. I've never been here."

He considered this. "In that case, come with me. I'll show you something."

She looked away, hesitant. He said, "I just want to show you something nice."

She picked up her satchel and followed him to a

trail that curved up a steep incline, first to the right and then to the left. She felt the strain in her calves as they climbed higher and higher. Finally, they came to a clearing around a bend. The young man stopped and said, "Look."

In the distance lay Prague, sparkling and magnificent under a pale blue sky streaked with white. From here it looked as if the entire city could rest in her palm. The battlements and bridges did not seem real. She could see the Stone Bridge but was too far away to make out the individual statues. Somewhere in the midst of those buildings was the squalid and crowded quarter, but from here the city resembled a single stone sculpture, a work of art.

"Should we sit down?" he asked.

Rivka sat near him on a patch of grass. If she turned to the left, she could see the panorama of hills and fields with the city, like a jewel, set in a crook of the river. She studied it to avoid looking at him.

He said, "Since you're not going to ask me any questions, I'll tell you that my name is Mikul Tomas. My father was a butcher in Freiberg, and my mother was the daughter of a peddler in Prague. My grandfather sold matches, mostly, but sometimes wooden toys. Or so I was told. He died before I was born. My parents had three sons before me, all of them dead of the plague. I was born here in Prague under a blighted star—"

She turned to him. "Why?"

He looked startled. "Why was I born in Prague?"

"No, why was your star blighted?"

"I don't know why it was blighted, I only know that it was."

"I mean, how do you know?"

"My father died when I was twelve. My mother died last year. Her illness left me in debt. I don't keep the money I earn. Most goes to my creditors. I missed the last two payments, and I may be in trouble again."

"I see," Rivka said, even though she wasn't quite sure what a creditor was. "You have no family at all?" She couldn't imagine being so alone in the world.

"I have family in Germany. I have an aunt and uncle and cousins. They wrote me a letter when my mother died and said I could go there."

"Why don't you?"

"I promised not to leave until I paid my debts. My uncle sent as much money as he could, but it wasn't enough. If I tried to leave and got caught—" He shook his head and didn't finish.

From the position of the sun, Rivka knew it was midafternoon. She wanted to be home before her mother returned, but she also wanted to stay and absorb the loveliness of the woods. It might be the last time she would visit the forest, and she must savor each moment so she could remember it all her life.

But the shadows of the trees were growing long. "I had better go now," she said. "Thank you so much for bringing me here."

"I'll walk back with you," Mikul replied.

Rivka followed him gratefully, realizing she might

not have found her way out of the forest so easily. Down, down, down, they walked until the ground leveled out. Now she could smell the dampness of the river nearby. At last they emerged from the trees and followed the road toward the city.

They were nearing the potato fields when Mikul stopped. A wagon with an official insignia drawn by two mules stood near the workers. Rivka felt a stab of fright—had they come for her, to take her to jail or back to the quarter in shame? She couldn't imagine how someone had figured out where she was.

Both she and Mikul watched as a uniformed man spoke to the foreman in the white muslin shirt. Mikul said, "It's the constable." She had the feeling he was as frightened as she.

Suddenly the foreman pointed toward them and cried, "There he is. That is Mikulase Tomas."

Mikul remained perfectly still. A few workers were looking their way as the constable, followed by two other men, dressed in the blue uniform of the city watchmen, came marching down the hill toward them. "Is your name Mikulase Tomas?" the constable asked.

"Yes, sir. That is my name."

"You are under arrest for debt," he said, taking out a rope to bind Mikul's hands. Mikul submitted, staring at the ground as if ashamed.

Rivka watched as the constable bound Mikul's hands and, with the other officers, escorted him to the wagon. She wanted to know what was happening but was too frightened to ask.

After the wagon rattled away, Rivka walked alone toward town. When she reached the marketplace, she asked a peddler where debtors were taken when they were arrested. The peddler looked at her as if she had asked the world's stupidest question.

"The debtors' prison," he said.

Rivka nodded as if she knew what that was. She turned and walked away. The marketplace was quieter at this hour of the afternoon. Bravely she approached a woman behind a pastry stall and said, "Excuse me, ma'am. Can you tell me where I will find the debtors' prison?" She didn't even have to remind herself to be bold and look the woman directly in the face. She was growing accustomed to acting like a boy.

"The prison's near the horse market at the bottom of the hill."

"Which direction?" Rivka asked.

The woman eyed Rivka strangely, as if everyone must know where the horse market was. She pointed and said, "That way." Rivka thanked her. She knew she should return home immediately, before her mother discovered that she was missing, but she felt she had to find out what had happened to Mikul.

She found the horse market near a main thoroughfare that was lined with shops and wide enough for several carriages side by side. She asked again about the prison and was directed to a squat limestone building with small, high windows no wider than a man's hand.

Rivka knew about bartering from the peddlers in the quarter. She took two coins from her satchel and put them in one pocket. She put one in another pocket. Then she knocked on the prison door.

A man opened the door. "What do you want?"

"I want to see someone here. Mikulase Tomas. He's in prison for debt."

"You can't see him. It's against the rules."

He started to close the door. Rivka said, "I can pay, sir. Not much, but I can pay."

He studied her. "What can you pay?"

"One zlatka."

"Two zlatky. You can talk to him for ten minutes. No more, or it's my hide in trouble."

"Yes, sir. Thank you, sir." She took the two coins from her pocket, careful to let him see that the pocket was then left empty.

The man led her down a corridor to a door, which he unlocked with a key. "Ten minutes," he said. She stepped inside, and he locked the door behind her. Mikul was standing in the darkness. The floor was covered with sawdust, and the only furnishings were a three-legged milk stool and a straw pallet.

"Hello," she said.

"Hello," he replied, looking as surprised as if a ghost had entered his cell.

She said, "I don't understand why you're here."

"I told you, I'm in debt. I missed my last two payments because of the rain. I didn't work for two weeks."

"But if you're locked up, how will you get the money?"

"So you understand the problem," he said. "I was here for six weeks in the winter because I couldn't find work. I told you I was born under a blighted star."

"What will you do?"

"Tomorrow morning I have a hearing with the magistrate. I will explain the situation. If I'm lucky, he will let me out again so I can work. If I'm not lucky, I'll have to serve a sentence."

"How much money do you need?"

"More than you have, I'm sure. Unless your secret is that you're an heiress in hiding and much richer than you look."

"I'm not an heiress. But I want to know how much."

"Three hundred zlatky."

He may as well have said a million. Three hundred zlatky was many weeks' work in the fields. Rivka was certain her father didn't have that much money, even though he did know how to raise funds among the Jews when it was needed.

"You see," he said. "I told you you couldn't help."

"But maybe I can."

In the shadows Mikul's face seemed older, his eyes sunken and sad. He pulled up the milk stool and said, "Here, sit down. Tell me who you are and how you think you can help me."

She lowered her voice to a whisper so the jailer wouldn't hear. "My name is Rivka Liebermann. I dressed like a boy so I could leave the Jewish quarter. I wanted to see what was outside—"

"You're Jewish?" He sounded incredulous.

She remembered all the stories she'd heard about how suspicious Christians were of Jews. "Do you think I should have horns?"

He smiled. "I've just never met anyone Jewish. Nobody told me Jewish girls were so pretty. How anyone can believe you're a boy, I don't know." He put out his hand. "We're friends, remember?"

Shyly Rivka took his hand, just for a moment, then pulled away.

He said, "So how can you help me? Do you have secret gold hidden away? I've heard that all the Jews have secret gold."

"That's not true—"

"Then tell me how you think you can help me."

"When I tell my father what has happened, how unfair this is—"

"Who is your father, and why should he help me? Three hundred zlatky is a lot of money."

"My father is a good man. He works hard for fair laws. He is a doctor and spends all his time helping people. When Jewish families have no place to live, he helps them find homes inside the quarter. Maybe he will help you. He helps everyone."

"Your father is a doctor?" There was genuine respect in his voice.

The door rattled open. "You've got to go now," the jailer said.

Mikul took a handful of oak chips from his pocket. "Can you get my wages tomorrow?"

Rivka took the chips and nodded. It was the least she could do.

8

The late afternoon sun was low in the sky. Soon the yellow lantern mounted on the arched stone portal leading from the prison to the street would be lit. An ache in Rivka's empty stomach reminded her that, except for the apple, she hadn't eaten all afternoon. She took the other apple from her satchel and ate it as she walked. Even with the apple, her stomach growled angrily. She wanted another.

In a main thoroughfare a bakery was still open, the lowered window forming a ledge displaying two loaves of bread and an apple tart. She wanted the apple tart but didn't dare eat something not prepared according to Jewish law. Instead, afraid to speak now that she knew her accent marked her as a foreigner, she moved to another window and pointed to a green apple. At any moment, she felt, someone would see through her disguise. Having just seen Mikul carted off to prison increased her fear. The very idea of being taken to jail or returned to the Jewish quarter in shame filled her with a fright so intense that she felt every shadow in the street was an officer coming for her.

She paid for the apple. The fruit seller, whose pudgy face reminded her of a potato, had gentle, sky blue eyes. How tempting it was to smile sweetly at him and say something, but she must take care.

The cobblestones underfoot were uneven. As she walked, she thought about how kind Mikul had been when he topped off her bag with potatoes. Surely a young man so generous didn't belong in prison. There simply had to be a mistake. How could the laws be so unfair? All Mikul had done, it seemed to her, was to take care of his sick mother. For that he was treated as a criminal. It was unconscionable. What kind of law would take him from his work in the fields and put him in prison for debt?

She simply could not let Mikul, who had been kind to her, sit in prison without help and without a friend. How good she felt to have a goal, a purpose, something large that she felt she must do. This must be how her father, a doctor of medicine and an influential man in the government of the Jewish quarter, felt all the time. This was how Jakob would feel when he became a rabbi and assumed a position of leadership in the community.

After ducking into an alley to change back into the overcoat and three-cornered hat, Rivka approached the gate and marched confidently past the guard. Once inside the quarter, she hurried home. The angels must indeed have been protecting her, because none of her neighbors were outside as she ran up the four flights of stairs and then climbed the last set to the roof. She quickly changed her clothes and then climbed down to the door leading to her bedroom.

Most amazing of all was that her mother had not yet returned home. Rivka hid her brothers' clothing in her chest and then went into the kitchen to start supper. She was slicing sweet beets when her mother came in.

Rivka listened attentively as her mother explained that cousin Vietka's health had taken a turn for the worse. Rivka's father, who was now tending him, believed Vietka's fever would be down by morning. Rivka's mother assumed her daughter had spent the afternoon at home. Rivka was startled—and uncomfortable—with how easy it was to deceive her mother.

The sun was setting when the boys' footsteps pounded up the stairs. Rivka's mother held still and drew in her breath, listening. Nothing would convince the boys to climb the stairs slowly and with care. Time and again their mother told them how many children were injured, and even killed, falling from such rickety stairs, but after a full day of sitting in Hebrew school, they were so glad to be out that their energy seemed boundless, and they always forgot to climb slowly.

Ahvram, the youngest, came bursting in the door, covered from shoes to knees with mud.

Rivka said, "How did you get so dirty? Come out here." To her mother, she said, "I'll get him cleaned up."

Rivka was on the stairs with Ahvram trailing behind when the Brandeis's window opened, and Friedl poked her head out. "Rivka! What were you doing dressed like a boy?"

Rivka looked back at her brother. "What are you talking about?" she said, feigning annoyance. "Stay here," she told Ahvram. She went to the window and whispered, "I'll tell you everything later, I promise. But please don't say anything to anyone. Promise?"

"I promise," said Friedl. "I'll see you tomorrow morning at the market. I'll wait for you."

"All right," Rivka replied. Friedl pulled her head back inside and closed the window.

That could certainly have turned into a disaster. Rivka held Ahvram's hand tightly as they walked down the rest of the stairs. On the street, she removed his shoes and socks and rolled up his trousers so she could wash his legs at the well. "You have to stop jumping in puddles, Ahvram," she said. "You're not a baby anymore."

"Were you dressed like a boy?"

"Of course not. Don't be silly. Come on."

Once they were back home, Rivka helped him change his clothes. Ahvram was scrubbed clean and fresh when the door opened and their father came in. He hung his overcoat on the peg by the door and then went into his room.

Rivka followed him. "Papa?" she said.

"Yes, Rivka?" he said absentmindedly as he took papers from his satchel.

"I heard about a Christian boy who was jailed unfairly."

"Mmm," he said, straightening the papers on the desk.

"It was unfair, Papa. He was put in debtors' prison

because he missed some payments. He's paying off the doctor from when his mother was dying."

"Such things happen out there. We have no such debtors' laws in our quarter. We treat those in debt more humanely and more sensibly."

"Can we help him, Papa?"

Now her father stopped what he was doing and looked at her, startled. "Impossible. The laws of the Christians do not concern us. We have enough trouble taking care of ourselves."

"But, Papa—"

"Do not think any more about this Christian boy. Do not even mention him."

The last sentence was a command, leaving Rivka with no choice but to say, "Yes, Papa."

"It is commendable that you want to help this boy. But trust me, Rivka, his troubles are none of your concern."

"Yes, Papa. It's just that the law is so unfair."

"Many of their laws are unfair, particularly to us. It is absurd to lock a man in prison because he cannot pay his debts. How can he pay them from prison? Be thankful that we are allowed to govern ourselves."

It was then that Rivka noticed her mother standing behind her in the doorway, listening to their discussion and looking curiously at Rivka. Her father hadn't thought to ask how she had heard about this Christian boy. But her mother might.

Rivka waited, feeling shaky, but all her mother said was, "Dinner is ready."

Rivka was silent during the meal, disappointed in

her father's response. Had Mikul been Jewish, her father would have certainly helped him. This seemed wrong to Rivka. She had complete faith that if her father wanted to help Mikul, he'd know how. He was an important man, after all. Twice he had been elected secretary to the Jewish council, and once he'd had a private audience with the Empress's officers to discuss laws affecting the Jews. The problem was he simply didn't want to help.

The idea that her father could err so deeply was disturbing. She had always been proud of his position of respect and his role as a revered doctor. Often people came to him to ask for medical and sometimes legal advice. He healed the sick, and in doing so, performed God's work. She was sometimes frightened of him, and he had always seemed larger than life to her, but she had never before doubted his wisdom and integrity.

Rivka had been taught that the Jews were the chosen people, and as such, they had a mission to humanity: to live as a light among nations, showing others the way to God. But how could they be a chosen people, a light among nations, if they closed their eyes to injustice? How could they be fit to uphold the ancient covenant if they did not try to correct unfairness wherever they found it? She wanted to tell her father what she was thinking, but she knew better. When he said he wanted a subject dropped, he meant it.

The boys chattered constantly through dinner.

"Papa," said Markus, "why was the full moon this month smaller than the full moon last month?" Rivka's father explained about the tilting of the earth and the changing distance of the moon. Markus's next question was about the Talmud story his class had studied that day. Their father answered it, as well.

Then Ahvram asked, "Is Mama going to die someday?" Ever since their grandfather died the summer before, death had been very much on Ahvram's mind. The recent death of the mother of one of his school friends had increased his anxiety.

Their father said, "Yes, one day. We all die one day. But your mother is healthy, so you have nothing to worry about now."

"But if Rivka goes away to get married and Mama dies," said Ahvram, "who will take care of me?"

"Mama's perfectly healthy," their father said.

"But when she does die," Ahvram said, "who will take care of me?"

Their mother said, "Am I looking that bad, Ahvram?" Rivka knew this was her mother's idea of a joke.

"But what will happen?" Ahvram asked.

Their father said, "You will not always need someone to take care of you. One day you'll be big like Jakob, and you'll take care of yourself."

Ahvram thought this over. He said, "But I need someone to take care of me." He set his fists down on the table, and Rivka suspected he was thinking about all the things he needed help with: he couldn't take a bath by himself, he still had trouble lacing his shoes, and he couldn't reach anything from the shelves near the stove.

Again, their father explained that their mother was healthy and that soon Ahvram would be old enough to take care of himself. Listening, Rivka knew her father was giving the wrong answer. His words, although logical, were simply not reassuring to Ahvram. Later she would talk to her brother herself.

They sang the after-dinner blessing, then Rivka and her mother washed the dishes. Ahvram stayed in the kitchen, near Rivka. "Is Rivka going to die one day, too?" he asked.

"What's all this with everyone dying?" their mother said. "I can understand your concern about me, but Rivka? She's fifteen years old, and except for her stomachaches, she's strong as an ox."

When Ahvram didn't answer, their mother said, "Everyone dies, Ahvram, but usually not when they are young and healthy. Rivka's young and healthy. She is going to be married soon."

Rivka put the spices back on the shelf. Her mother didn't understand Ahvram's fears, either. This realization was as startling as the fact that her mother didn't know where Rivka had been all afternoon.

Bedtime came, and Rivka was helping Ahvram into his nightshirt. Markus and Nathan were on Nathan's side of the bed, arguing, and Rivka's parents were in the next room, out of hearing distance.

Rivka whispered, "Ahvram, there will always be someone to take care of you."

He said, "But if Mama dies, and if you go away, *who* will take care of me?"

"Before Mama dies, she will appoint someone to take care of you."

Ahvram looked at her, as if assessing the truth of what she said. "Do you promise?"

"I promise. Before Mama dies she will give some-one the important task of taking care of Ahvram. I will make sure of that, too. And so will Papa." She repeated once again for emphasis, "There will *always* be someone to take care of you."

He seemed vastly reassured. How startling that Rivka understood how to soothe his fear, whereas her father and mother had not. She was touched by the childishness of Ahvram's concerns—he was wor-ried about his own well-being, not his mother's and not his sister's.

Later, in her own bed, after all the candles had been put out, Rivka thought she had indeed told Ahvram the truth. There would always be someone to take care of him. He would never be left alone in a jail cell without people working to free him. Should a Jew fall into such trouble, as Jews often did, the entire community would work to rescue him. This didn't mean, of course, that they would succeed. Rivka had heard enough stories of the atrocities Jews suffered to know that. But at least there would be people who cared.

Footsteps came toward Rivka's room. She sat up and waited. Maybe it was her father, sensing her unease. But no, it was her mother, come to kiss her good-night. She kissed Rivka's cheek and said, "I do not know how I will bear it when you marry Oskar Kara. The house will be so empty without you."

"My wedding is months away, Mama."

"When you are married, Rivka, this anxiety of yours will go away, I promise. You will be happy with Oskar Kara. Trust me."

"Yes, Mama."

"Now, Rivka, listen closely. I never want you to mention that Christian boy again. Do you understand?"

"But, Mama, the law is unfair. How can we not help when we know someone is in trouble?"

"He will be able to take care of himself. Is he strong? Can he work? Why are you so worried about him? We are the ones who suffer from unfair laws. We never know when we will be attacked again. If you understood their laws, you would know that we are the ones who have to worry, not a healthy and strong Christian boy."

"But, Mama—" She had thought her parents would help her, but they wouldn't even let her explain.

"But nothing. Go to sleep." Her mother kissed her cheek again and left.

Now what would Rivka do with Mikul's oak chips? She couldn't keep his full day's earnings, especially when he was in prison for debt. Should she try once more to talk to her parents? No, they had told her not to mention Mikul again, and a parental order was as binding as any law. This left her with a painful choice: risk leaving the quarter in disguise a third time or keep Mikul's money when he needed it so badly. Keeping Mikul's money was wrong. If she did as her parents wanted, she would be ignoring their years of teaching. A woman's greatest virtue was her compassion and her willingness to help others, and helping Mikul was the right and compassionate thing to do.

Rivka was at the kitchen table the following morning rolling out pastry crust when two sharp knocks came at the door. Chavele always knocked twice, hard. "I'll answer it," Rivka called to her mother, who was in the boys' bedroom.

Chavele, her hair entirely hidden by a scarf, was holding an empty market basket. Instead of inviting her in, Rivka stepped outside and closed the door. "I have to tell you something," she whispered. "Can we sit here?"

Chavele sat down beside Rivka on the landing. It had been almost two weeks since Rivka had seen her. There had been a time, before Chavele had married and moved out of the building, when Rivka had seen her every day. Chavele had been as familiar as a sister.

Chavele said, "I have something to tell you, too. But you first."

"I went outside, by myself."

"Outside the quarter?"

Rivka saw an expression of disapproval in Chavele's face. It occurred to her that since Chavele had married, she had grown even more timid. She seemed plump as well, more filled out and bustier, even matronly in her scarf. How was it that Chavele had gone so quickly from a girl to looking like a woman?

"I went twice," Rivka said, "dressed as a boy. I wanted to see for myself. The first time I went was on Tuesday. I said I was quilting with you."

"Don't do it again," said Chavele. "Don't go out anymore, and don't use my name. Oh, Rivka." Chavele gripped the railing as if to steady herself. "Think how dangerous it is. If you got caught, what would your parents do? And what would Oskar Kara say?"

"I know, but I had to go. I had to."

"All right, you went. But don't do it again, Rivka. Please. Be sensible."

Rivka wanted to explain how she had felt in the forest, so close to God, and what she had thought of walking through the marketplace dressed as a boy. She also wanted to tell Chavele about Mikul's oak chips. But Chavele's expression, which had always struck Rivka as sweet, now seemed distant and preoccupied. So instead Rivka changed the subject. "Tell me your news."

Chavele smiled. The yellow flecks in her eyes glistened, as if reflecting candlelight. "I am going to have a baby." She put her hand to her belly.

"A baby!" The words of congratulations came naturally. "Mazel tov, Chavele. That's wonderful!" Rivka smiled, but what she felt was the sharp and familiar ache in her stomach. Her chest constricted painfully. Soon she would be married to Oskar Kara, and soon she would have a baby, too. But why should this thought disturb her so? Look how happy Chavele was, glowing with her news.

Rivka stood up. "We must tell my mother. She'll be so happy." Rivka opened the door and led Chavele inside. After hearing the news, her mother made a fuss over Chavele, insisting that she sit down, asking questions and giving advice. Through it all, her mother never even thought to ask about the quilting on Tuesday. Rivka supposed that if her mother had asked, Chavele would have lied for her this once, since Rivka had promised never to put her in such a position again.

"I can't stay," Chavele said, getting up from the table. "I have to go to the candlemaker now." They said their good-byes, and Rivka and her mother came out on the landing and watched as Chavele walked down the stairs, turning often to wave at them.

Just then Friedl, who must have heard the commotion, opened the window facing the stair. "Do you want to go to the market now, Rivka? My mother needs beef for supper."

"Go ahead," said Rivka's mother. "We need onions. Get some salt, too."

Rivka took the shopping basket from the peg over the kitchen cupboard. She counted out a few coins from the dish her mother kept on the window sill, then went to join Friedl on the stairs.

As soon as they reached the street, Friedl started in. "All right, what were you doing dressed as a boy? Dubra saw you, too, but she didn't recognize you. You're lucky she didn't because she would have told everyone by now."

"Friedl, please don't tell anyone."

Friedl stopped at the seriousness of Rivka's tone. "What were you doing?" she demanded.

So Rivka told her everything. She told her about her disguise and the first day harvesting potatoes. She told her about Mikul and about how she had seen him the second day, when she had visited the forest. Then she told her about how Mikul was in jail and how she had promised to redeem his oak chips.

When she finished, Friedl said, "I guess you have to go again."

"Will you help me think of a way so nobody will miss me? I only need to go for a few hours."

"I guess so. I plan to visit my cousin this afternoon. You can say you're with me."

Thank goodness someone understood. It was comforting to have Friedl to talk to, especially with Jakob gone. Just then, Rivka missed Jakob terribly. If he were here, she imagined he would say she had to do what she knew was right and trust that all would turn out well.

9

Rivka was sweeping the kitchen floor when Friedl knocked. She knew it was Friedl from the three light taps. "I'll get it," she said to her mother, who was straightening her room.

When Rivka opened the door, Friedl said loudly enough for Rivka's mother to hear, "Rivka, can you come down? I'm going to my cousin's."

"Mama," said Rivka, "may I go?"

"Go," called her mother.

Rivka shouted good-bye. On her way out the door, she tapped her waistband to make sure Mikul's oak chips and her money were safe.

Once on the landing, Rivka whispered, "I have to get my bundle. Wait here."

As quietly as she could manage, she climbed the stairs to the roof to retrieve the bundle of clothing she had hidden there earlier. When she returned, Friedl said, "Are you really going to do this?"

"What can I do?" said Rivka. "Keep his money?"

When they reached the street, Rivka said, "I need a place to change."

"Here." Friedl ducked into a narrow alley. "Nobody will see you if I stand right here."

When Rivka had put on the trousers and the coat

with the patch and tucked her braids under the three-cornered hat, Friedl said, "You look like a boy. If nobody looks too closely."

"Let's hope nobody does," said Rivka. She carefully put the coins and the oak chips in a pocket of the Czech-style jacket.

When they neared Široká, Rivka said, "I should go by myself. I won't be more than three hours, I promise."

"All right. Be careful," said Friedl.

Rivka, on her own again, marched confidently through the gate, and for the third time passed into the larger city. As before, she experienced a soaring sensation of freedom. She tried to imagine what life would be like if she could pass through the gate anytime she chose. She found a hiding place and changed into the shorter jacket without the patch. Then she headed toward the main part of the city. A woman walked ahead of her with a basket on her arm. Two yellow hounds sniffed curiously at Rivka's heels, then trotted off into an alley. Just a few days ago, Prague was vast and incomprehensible, an endless tangle of streets and alleys. Now that some of the streets were familiar, the city seemed to be shrinking.

Her first task was to redeem Mikul's chips. She crossed the Stone Bridge and hurried along, not pausing in any of the market areas or looking into any shopwindows. She had no time to waste.

The smell of the river reminded her of the hours she had spent in the forest the day before, and she wished she had time to return to the woods. Longingly, she remembered how the light had slanted through the trees and how spongy the moss had felt underfoot, but all she could do was steal furtive looks at the hills and march onward.

A different man was in charge at the potato fields. He was heavier, with a bulbous nose. She approached him and said, "Excuse me, sir." From a distance of four paces she could smell a sour scent like stale wine clinging to his clothing.

She took the oak chips from her pocket. "I have come to redeem Mikulase Tomas's chips for him."

"He's still in prison?"

"Yes, sir." At least she supposed Mikul was still in prison.

The man took the chips and gave her seven coins.

"Thank you, sir," she said. She put the coins into her pocket and walked back toward the river.

To reach the prison she crossed the Stone Bridge and walked eastward. At the prison, she knocked on the door. As before, the guard demanded two zlatky before permitting her inside.

"Never mind," she said. Two zlatky was too much. She walked around the outside of the prison and found four windows set high in the wall. "Mikul?" she called.

An older man's voice, which certainly wasn't Mikul's, called out mockingly, "Mikul! Mikul!"

Rivka ignored him and called again, "Mikul?"

This time Mikul answered. "Hey, is that you? You

came back!" He hoisted himself to one of the windows, probably by standing on the milk stool. "See that barrel over there?" he said. "Can you roll it over?"

The barrel, lying on its side, was in an alley across the street. Although empty, it was heavy and clattered noisily across the cobblestones. After rolling it under Mikul's window, Rivka heaved it upright. That done, she climbed on top and stood with her face almost even with the window.

The window was so narrow she could see only the middle half of Mikul's face. He said, "So are you an angel sent by God to help me?"

"I'm no angel. I'm just an ordinary girl who—"

Mikul laughed. "You're no ordinary girl. Ordinary girls don't dress up like boys and leave the Jewish quarter on their own. Ordinary girls don't care about getting strangers out of prison."

"How long do you have to stay here?"

"Just until the morning. I got lucky with the new magistrate. I signed a paper swearing I will not leave Prague until my debt is paid. The magistrate will let me out so I can work, because the only payments I missed were due to the weather."

"Here is your money," she said.

Mikul made no motion to take it. "If I keep it here," he whispered, "they'll take it away from me. The jailer will think up some fine or penalty. I have to hide it until I can give it to my creditors. Can you hold it for me?"

"I can't," she said. "I have to go home, and I don't know if I will be able to come out again."

Even more quietly, he said, "If I give you the key to my room, will you put the money inside?"

She hesitated. The idea of going to Mikul's room frightened her. She said, "I have to go back. My mother doesn't know I'm gone."

He let his breath out in a deep sigh and looked off into the distance. She imagined he was trying to think of another way to keep his money safe. She said, "Maybe I can take it to your room, if it isn't too far."

He brightened. "It isn't far at all. You don't have to bring my key back to me. Just slide it under the door after you lock it. I will ask the landlord to let me in."

He handed her the key, which was heavy and filled her hand. Holding it made her feel as though she had taken a step in a new and frightening direction, as if she were about to enter forbidden ground.

Mikul leaned forward and whispered, "In front of the cupboard in my room is a loose floorboard. Put the money underneath."

"All right."

"It's number nineteen Panská Street, room six. Go that way," he said, pointing. "After a few blocks, you'll see Panská Street."

"All right."

He asked, "Do Jews believe in angels?"

"We have the synagogue angels. Why?"

"What do they look like?"

"I don't know. Nobody has ever seen them."

He blinked, surprised. "Then how do you know they're there?"

Now Rivka was surprised. Then she remembered that he was Christian and therefore believed God's portrait could be painted. He probably also believed angels were statues made of stone. "We know they're there because they have been protecting the synagogue for hundreds of years. No one has ever seen God, either, but we know He's there because He protects the Jews."

"Does He, Rivka? I'm sorry to ask this, but then why does He let the Jews be locked up in a walled ghetto?"

The answer, which she had heard many times, came to her easily. "Our suffering is part of God's plan. In the end, we will be redeemed. The Messiah will come, and the ten lost tribes will be gathered from exile, and all the Jews will march in a mighty army to place the Messiah on King David's throne in Jerusalem."

Mikul stared at her. Her response had evidently dazed him. "I see," he said. Rivka had the feeling, though, that he didn't.

"I had better go," she said.

"Yes," he said, but he seemed uncertain. She stood there a moment longer but couldn't think of anything else to say. Then she jumped down from the barrel and headed in the direction he had pointed. Just before she was out of sight, she turned and waved.

Number 19 Panská Street was a plain structure,

two stories high, nestled between two larger buildings. The brick was soft red and crumbling. The window shutters, which long ago must have been painted red, were chipped and faded to pink.

The front door was unlocked and led to a windowless corridor. On each side of the corridor were two doors numbered with faded black paint. At the end of the corridor was a narrow staircase. Mikul's room, Rivka assumed, must be upstairs. Her guess proved correct. Room 5 stood at the top of the staircase to the right. Opposite was room 6.

She unlocked Mikul's door and went in. Inside was a room with a slanted ceiling supported by heavy beams. To the right of the door was a single window facing the street. In the dim light, the walls seemed dingy gray. Pushed against the left wall was a bed with a mattress. Next to the bed was a wooden table with a wash basin. Along the opposite wall was a low bench on which Mikul's clothes were folded: a few extra shirts, a pair of trousers, two pairs of socks. A shelf dug into the thickness of the wall contained a few ceramic bowls, one badly chipped, and a stack of papers and letters tied with string.

Rivka stood as if transfixed, taking in this utterly alien room. How lonely Mikul must be. How stark and bare his life was: waking up alone with nobody to talk to, going out into the fields to work all day, turning his money over to his creditors, spending time in prison when he missed his payments. She could see that Mikul didn't live a magical life simply because he was born outside the quarter. People suffered out here just as much as they did in the quarter, or—the thought startled her, but looking around the room, what else could she think?—perhaps even more.

From the street came the creaking of wagon wheels and the shouting of peddlers. The sounds were familiar, much like the noises on the streets in the quarter. At the same time, everything was strangely different, the way Rivka felt when she saw her reflection in a distorted mirror. Here the cries were in Czech only; the language in the quarter was mostly Yiddish mixed with Czech and German words and phrases. Out here it seemed as if there was an echo in the streets, as if the sounds here traveled farther.

In front of the cupboard she found the loose board. She lifted it up and set the coins inside in an empty dish. Then she took her own money from her pocket and put it in the dish as well. Mikul needed it more than she did. She replaced the board. Now she had to get home quickly, before anyone discovered her missing. She didn't know how long it had been since she and Friedl had parted—at least two hours. She changed into the three-cornered hat and the overcoat with the patch. She was in a hurry, so she would just have to walk back to the gate in Jewish clothing. She thought she would be safe. Her father went out often, after all.

She went into the corridor, locked the door, and then slipped the key under the door. She walked as quickly as she dared toward the quarter. She arrived at the gate to find the Jewish guard standing just inside, deep in conversation with a peddler. Neither of them looked up as she passed by.

Then she was back inside, hurrying toward Friedl's cousin's building. She ducked into a narrow alley and crouched behind a barrel to change into her own clothes. Nothing, she knew, could be more foolish than what she was doing at that very moment. She paused at the base of the stairs to catch her breath, then ran lightly up the three flights to Friedl's cousin's home.

Friedl herself answered the door. "It's about time," she said.

Rivka stood just inside the door as Friedl said good-bye. She could scarcely manage to smile sweetly at Friedl's cousin, as was expected of her. She was still out of breath, and her heart was thumping.

When Rivka and Friedl were back in the street, Friedl said, "Did you give him his money?"

"Yes," Rivka said.

"Well?"

Friedl asked for details, but Rivka didn't want to reveal that she had visited Mikul's room, which had been like peeking into the most personal part of his life. All she said was, "I redeemed his chips and then brought his money to the jail."

"It sure took you long enough."

"I had to do a lot of walking."

"Now it's all done," Friedl said. "You don't need to have anything more to do with him."

10

Rivka entered the kitchen and found a note from her mother on the table. She had written that she was downstairs visiting Rivka's grandmother and would be back soon. With a quill from her father's desk Rivka added: "I am up on the roof, Mama."

She sat in her favorite spot on the mat in the corner directly in front of her flower pots. Sitting here permitted her to see over the quarter walls to the hills beyond. If she turned and looked to the left, she could see stored cleaning supplies: buckets with scrub brushes, a long-handled rag mop, and a straw broom. If she stood up, she could see the neighboring rooftops with clotheslines and clothes snapping in the breeze like so many motley and colorful flags. The rooftop itself felt dusty, dingy.

She looked between two buildings to where she could see a small stretch of the hills beyond. Her father thought Jakob's fairy tales had created her restlessness, but sitting here Rivka understood the problem was this one window to the outside world. She'd seen enough to make her curious. Well, now she had gone. She'd had her adventure, her sweet and precious secret. There was no reason to go again. She must learn to be happy about her upcoming marriage.

Rivka heard creaking on the stairs, and then the sound of their door opening and closing. Soon it would be time to begin supper. She and her mother would go to bed early that night, as they always did on Thursdays. Friday was the busiest day of the week for them, and for all the other women in the quarter. Food would have to be prepared for the day of rest and the entire house made ready for Sabbath.

Next morning, Rivka and her mother went early to the marketplace, each with an empty basket on her arm. "We need beef and soap," said Rivka's mother. They turned the corner to the open market and saw long lines everywhere. "We should have come sooner," she said. The longest line, for the butcher's shop, reached into the street, with women holding baskets or burlap shopping bags.

Her mother spent a few minutes greeting people and then said, "Rivka, you stand in the butcher's line. I'm going to the soapmaker."

"Yes, Mama."

Soon Rivka heard a delighted squeal behind her. Someone said, "Rivka Liebermann!" She turned and saw Dobrisch, Chavele's oldest sister. Dobrisch carried an infant in a cloth carrier on her back, and she held the hand of a small girl of no more than two or three.

Dobrisch said, "We heard your news last night. My husband heard from Moshe Bassevi, who heard from Oskar Kara's cousin that you will be engaged! Is it true, Rivka? You will marry Oskar Kara?"

"It is true," Rivka said. Dobrisch let go of her toddler's hand and came forward to hug Rivka. "Mazel tov. I can just imagine how happy your mother is. When is the wedding?"

"In a few months."

A woman in front of Rivka, whom Rivka had seen several times in the marketplace but didn't know, turned and said, "So you are the girl marrying Oskar Kara? I wondered who it was."

Rivka had the sensation that the woman was looking at her with a new respect. How strange this all was. She had the feeling everyone in line was watching her. From far back in the line came a call. "Rivka, hello!"

Rivka stood on tiptoe and saw her aunt Perl, her mother's youngest sister. "Congratulations, dear," her aunt called.

"Thank you," she replied.

What she saw next gave her such a start that she felt faint. Standing on the corner near a red sandstone building and watching the entire scene was Mikul.

Instantly she looked away and turned to Dobrisch. "How is the baby?" she asked.

Dobrisch talked about the infant's latest illness, and Rivka pretended to listen. She nodded attentively, smiling her best smile, all the while wondering if she had imagined Mikul standing there, like a wisp of a dream or a spirit from one of Jakob's fairy tales come to play mischief with her life. Surely it was impossible that Mikul was standing in the Jewish marketplace on a busy Friday morning.

Dobrisch said, "What will you wear for the wedding? Will you make a new dress?"

"I don't know," Rivka said.

Her aunt Perl, who had come up to join them, said, "She is going to wear the dress her aunt Sarah wore. It was made from French lace for Rivka's grandmother. We had it taken in to fit Sarah, and Rivka is just her size. The dress is the most beautiful any bride has ever worn."

Rivka stole another peek in Mikul's direction. Yes, it was he. He wore an oversized coat and a German cap that entirely covered his hair. He was watching her. She hoped he would know not to say a word to her. If any of these women discovered that she had befriended a young Christian man, the word would quickly spread, and Rivka would have to answer some extremely embarrassing questions.

Young Gentile men, Rivka knew, often came into the quarter. Much to her father's annoyance, they frequented Jewish taverns, mostly on Sundays when taverns were closed in the larger city. They felt free to come whenever they wanted. The guards let them in because the tavern owners were happy to have their business. Nobody would think much of Mikul's presence. Rivka supposed he had covered his head to be politely inconspicuous.

When her mother returned from the soapmaker, more and more women came forward to congratulate Rivka. Fortunately her mother answered for her, saving her the necessity of speaking. Rivka's mother graciously accepted the congratulations and good wishes. "Of course we are delighted with the match," she said. Rivka knew she was trying to be humble, but anyone could see she was glowing with pride.

In her peripheral vision, she saw Mikul enter the dry-goods store. When he emerged, the line had shrunk, and Rivka and her mother were inside the butcher shop near the counter. Rivka watched as he sat across the square on a bench. He smoothed a sheet of paper on his lap and with a piece of charcoal began to write. Evidently he realized that he couldn't approach her and instead had decided to write her a note. But how on earth would he get the note to her? And what was he writing?

Finally it was their turn to be waited on. While her mother explained to the butcher how she wanted her meat carved, Rivka wandered outside. She stood by the door, pretending to ignore Mikul, who was still on the bench. When he walked toward the butcher shop, she turned away, sensing he was going to put the note in her basket. She held perfectly still and waited. Sure enough, she felt the motion as he dropped the note into her basket.

He stepped into the store and pretended to look around. Then he was gone. She turned around as nonchalantly as she could manage to see if anyone had noticed what Mikul had done, but nobody seemed to be paying attention. She reached into the basket and found the paper, which he had folded tightly. She tucked it safely into her waistband. How startling and strange that she and a Christian man could so easily be conspirators.

Her mother came out, and they walked on together. Next they stopped to buy potatoes from an open stall and then went to the baker in the next block. On their way home, her mother breathed deeply, looked up at the sky, and said, "What a perfectly lovely day!"

Surprised, Rivka looked at her mother and saw that she was flushed a lovely pink. "It has been less than two weeks since Jakob left," her mother went on. "I didn't think I could feel happy while he was away. I imagined I would have a weight in my heart every minute. There is nothing like a daughter's engagement to raise a mother's spirits."

Back at home, Rivka and her mother went quietly about their tasks, first cleaning each room from top to bottom, then baking tarts for dessert. Frequently throughout the day, Rivka patted her waistband where she had tucked Mikul's note, waiting for a safe opportunity to read it.

Later in the afternoon, her mother went to visit Mrs. Brandeis. Rivka, alone, climbed the ladder to the roof and sat down in her corner facing the hills. She took out Mikul's note and unfolded it. It read:

> *I don't feel right taking your money. I never take charity. Mostly I want to tell you that I know of another place even better than the one I showed you. I will wait for you every morning at sunup at the foot of the Stone Bridge on the side nearest the quarter. I hope you come.*
>
> *M.*

The note was even more dangerous than she had feared. Thank goodness nobody had seen it. He hadn't addressed her by name or signed his own. She wondered if he had done this to make it easier for her to deny knowledge of him had she gotten caught.

She couldn't leave the quarter again, that she knew. She had done what she wanted to do: she had been outside and had seen the city and forest for herself. Now she had to remember her duty to her family. She tore his note into pieces so small that nobody would ever know it had once been a shocking letter. Then she stood up and let the breeze take the pieces of paper and scatter them over the alley, four floors below. She heard the door close downstairs and knew her mother had returned, but the pain was back in her stomach, and she wanted some more time to herself. She recounted all the reasons she should not leave the quarter again and tried to relax so the ache would go away.

When she went back inside, the scent of the apple tarts filled the kitchen. The smell, heavy and sweet, turned Rivka's stomach. Her mouth watered, and her head felt light. "Mama, I feel sick," she said.

"Rivka, *what* is the matter." It was a command instead of a question.

"I don't know, Mama." But her stomach was turning, and the room spun dizzily. She ran to the ceramic basin and vomited. Her mother might be irritated, but she couldn't deny that Rivka was genuinely sick.

"My head hurts, Mama."

Her mother came over to her and cupped her

hand on Rivka's forehead. "You have no fever. Lie down. I'll get your father."

Rivka lay on her bed while her mother went to fetch her shawl. Then the door opened and closed, and her mother was gone. For a long time Rivka was alone, her head throbbing like a painful heartbeat. Her father would be out of patience. It annoyed him that he, a doctor, should have a daughter with such mysterious and unpredictable symptoms.

Sometime later her parents returned. Her father sat beside her and touched her stomach to locate the pain. Then he asked her to describe her headache. She said, "There's a pounding, Papa. I feel dizzy. And the light hurts my eyes."

"Rivka," he said, "I don't know what is wrong with you."

"My head hurts," she said.

Rivka's mother, in the tone she used when she was deeply upset, said, "My daughter is about to be married—not just married, but married to a man who is practically a prince. And what does she do? She gets sick, that's what she does."

"Let her spend the evening resting," said her father. "She'll be fine."

Saturday, as always, was quiet. Her father spent most of the day at the synagogue. Markus, he said, was getting old enough to join him for part of the afternoon. Rivka's stomach felt more settled by then, but she didn't speak much. Ahvram wanted her to play a game of sticks-and-pebbles, but she told him she needed to rest. In a large basket in a corner was a pile of her brothers' clothing waiting to be mended, and in another basket was a half-woven cloth, but today was the Sabbath, and all such tasks must wait.

Often on Saturdays she and her mother sat together on the bench with a blanket over their legs, talking about their family and neighbors and what news there was of Jews abroad. Today, though, Rivka's mother, who was seated at the table with a cup of cider, seemed to be deliberately leaving her daughter to her own thoughts.

Outside, the streets were quiet. No shops were open, and no peddlers were crying their wares. All the market stalls were shut tight. The only people on the street were men in their tall black hats, walking toward the synagogue in small groups, greeting each other with friendly smiles.

Two pearl gray pigeons had nested in the eaves just outside their front window. Rivka, sitting in her room, listened to their cooing, then opened the door to the outside to watch them. The pigeons, not knowing or caring that today was a holy day of rest, were busy at play, chasing each other, then swooping down and disappearing.

Rivka knew what she wanted. She wanted to go outside once more. She looked into the sky and thought about the forest and Mikul and wondered why she was tempted. Was she the only girl in the world cursed with this restlessness?

The pigeons reappeared and then flew over the buildings. As she watched them, she made a bargain with herself. She decided she would go out once more, only once more, and that would be all. Mikul had offered to take her to an even lovelier place to view the city than the one he had already shown her. How could she not take advantage of so lovely an opportunity?

She would leave on Monday, which would give her enough time to think of an alibi. She would beg Friedl to help her. She didn't dare go Tuesday on the pretence of visiting Chavele—not after Chavele had forbade her to use her name again.

That evening Rivka went downstairs to visit the Brandeises. She and Friedl sat in the kitchen closet. "I have to go out one more time," said Rivka. "I just want to."

"But, Rivka—"

"Please don't ask me any questions."

Friedl thought this over and then said, "Tomorrow I will spend with my grandmother."

"I'll say I was with you. Please? I'll come back by noon."

"Rivka, what if people find out?"

"They won't. I'll be careful."

Friedl hesitated. Then she said, "All right. But only if you tell me everything later. You have to tell me why you are going and what you are doing."

"I will," Rivka said. She hoped that by the time

she returned, she would understand what she was doing fully enough to explain it to someone else.

On Sunday, during the moments she could spare from her chores, Rivka secretly assembled her brothers' clothing. She was filled with fears and misgivings. That night, when her mother came to tell her goodnight, Rivka said, "Mama, may I visit with Friedl and her grandmother in the morning? I want to go early, for breakfast."

"So you're feeling better?"

"Yes, Mama."

Her mother looked uncertain but said, "All right."

Sometime in the night, Rivka awoke, trembling. She had dreamed that she and a man with dark hair were under the Stone Bridge at sunset, bathing together. They were laughing and splashing each other the way her brothers splashed each other in the bath when they were younger. Suddenly the man grew serious and pulled her into his arms.

She woke up with the sensation of the man's wet, cool flesh against hers. She thought the man in her dream had been Oskar because of his black hair. Then she thought he must have been Mikul, because why on earth would Oskar be under the Stone Bridge at sunset?

She had trouble falling back asleep.

11

Rivka, experienced now with sneaking through the gate, felt more at ease marching past the guard in her brothers' clothing. Once she was out of the quarter she changed into her jacket and cap and walked along, looking people square in the face, holding herself tall, walking with a strong, purposeful stride. Boys' clothes, she decided, made her feel powerful.

She reached the Stone Bridge just after sunup. Mikul was waiting for her at the foot of the bridge. She could see from the dampness of his clothing that he had bathed, probably in the river.

He smiled as she approached. "You came," he said.

His damp hair and the nearness of the river reminded Rivka of her dream. Her cheeks flushed, and she turned away, embarrassed. They walked side by side along the riverbank toward the city's outskirts. Even with the confidence she felt dressed as a boy, she still couldn't look at him. If Mikul noticed this, he didn't seem to mind.

He stopped when he saw a broken vegetable cart in the reeds. "Wait here," he said. He stepped through the weeds, hoisted the cart over his shoulders, and carried it back to the road. He set the cart down and studied it. "No," he said. "The bottom is rotted."

"No, what?" she asked.

"If the bottom weren't rotted, I could fix this and use it. I'd be able to pick apples in the forest and sell them for extra money."

"You're very resourceful." She wondered what it must be like to live all alone, scavenging for a living like a pigeon. Mikul seemed to think nothing of it.

"I've had to be resourceful," he replied. She thought he sounded proud of himself. He put the cart back in the reeds.

They continued along the river, walking through the farthest market square. Three Jewish men entered the marketplace from the north. They were dressed differently from Czech Jews: from their heavy over-coats and tall fur-lined hats, Rivka guessed they were from somewhere in the east. They didn't wear yellow patches, probably because nobody had yet told them the law in Prague. She heard them, in heavily accented Czech, asking directions to the Jewish quarter. Three young boys ridiculed the men, running in circles around them, threatening to pull their beards. A woman selling matches stared at them and said, "Ridiculous-looking yids."

Rivka watched, then turned away, uneasy. This was the closest she had come to understanding her mother's reluctance to leave the safety of the quarter. Why should the Jews put themselves in the way of hostility when they could stay safely at home?

Mikul noticed Rivka staring at the scene and said, "They have no reason to hate the Jews. They just do it out of habit. Or because everyone else does."

"How can they hate without reason?" Rivka asked.

"It's easy to hate people you don't know."

"I guess Friedl was right. People out here don't like us."

"They're just being stupid," Mikul said. "They don't know any better."

They were soon out of the city. Overhead, heavy white clouds moved swiftly, at times blocking the sun completely. Right now the sunshine streaked through the clouds and lit up the grass and trees. Rivka liked the moody and changeable sky.

A girl was coming down the road toward them, her blouse tied with a bright red ribbon, her hair in braids. Rivka had the feeling, from the way he drew himself up taller, that Mikul knew this girl.

When the girl was just a few paces away, they all three stopped. The girl smiled at Mikul and said, "I heard you were in jail. So what law did you break? Did you take advantage of helpless girls?"

As she made this startling speech, she glanced coyly at Mikul, then quickly looked down. She glanced at Rivka, then back at the ground again. Only then did Rivka remember that she was dressed as a boy.

Mikul shifted his weight to his other foot. Rivka had the feeling he was embarrassed. The silence went on too long. The girl smiled, as if she enjoyed teasing him. When at last he spoke, his voice sounded tight. "Greetings, Lara."

"Who's your friend?" As Lara asked this question, she continued to watch Mikul.

Mikul didn't seem to know how to answer. Rivka let her voice drop in timbre and said, "I'm Sebastian Gunther," but the girl didn't look at her again. She was evidently more interested in Mikul, for whom she flashed another smile.

"Um," Mikul stammered. Rivka expected him to smile back at Lara. Was he shy? Didn't men always react favorably when talked to that way by girls? He shifted his weight again and said, "We'd better get going. Good seeing you, Lara."

"Good seeing you," she said with a lilt in her voice, and she continued on her way.

Mikul picked up a walking stick, and then he and Rivka resumed walking. Rivka wondered if that was how she appeared when she smiled at Oskar Kara. "Never look a man directly in the eyes," her mother had told her. "This is too bold, and men do not like bold girls." Rivka knew how to look down and let her lashes quiver as if she were all aflutter with gentle emotion. She thought she knew how to do this better than Lara.

"You don't like her," Rivka finally said.

"She makes me uncomfortable." Then, after a pause, Mikul added, "I like you better."

His declaration should have made her feel strange or uncomfortable, but he had spoken in a simple, matter-of-fact tone, and she didn't feel the slightest unease. "Thank you," she said, feeling that her response was inadequate. How surprising that Mikul should like her even though she was behaving like a boy. She wondered if Oskar would want to marry her if he saw her as Mikul had.

They spent the early part of the morning climbing the tallest hill on the outskirts of the city. Rivka concentrated hard on every sight and smell, on the texture of each woodland plant, on the blue of the sky when the clouds parted. She wanted to be able to remember everything about this day forever and ever.

They climbed so high that Rivka was sure they couldn't climb any farther, that soon they would be in the clouds. Then Mikul stopped and said, "Look."

Framed by an arch of tree branches was a view of the city that took Rivka's breath away. Prague was so far away that the only structure she could identify was the castle high on its hill, shrouded in a light mist.

For a long time she stood, transfixed. Then Mikul sat down on a boulder, and she sat beside him. The boulder was so large that her feet barely touched the ground. The sunlight slanted through the branches of the trees surrounding them and set the treetops aglow. Mikul pointed to the wall of sunbeams and said, "It's like the light in a cathedral."

"It's beautiful," she said.

Mikul swung his feet, tapping his heels against the boulder. His movements reminded her of Nathan and made him seem younger. Then he startled her by saying, "Do you have brothers or sisters?"

The question jarred her. She looked at the city

and thought that somewhere there, studying their Hebrew letters, were Markus, Nathan, and Ahvram. From this distance she couldn't see the walls of the Jewish quarter or the world locked within, teeming with life.

"I have four brothers," she replied.

"Which is your favorite?"

That was easy. "Jakob. Everyone loves Jakob. He is the best scholar in the entire quarter and a great favorite among the rabbis. I have heard them predict that one day he will be as great as Rabbi Loew."

"Who is Rabbi Loew?"

The question surprised her. She had assumed that everyone knew of Rabbi Loew. "He was the greatest rabbi Prague has ever had. He was wise and had magical powers. Don't you know about the golem?"

"I have never heard of the golem." Mikul sounded apologetic.

So Rivka told Mikul about the golem, an artificial man created by Rabbi Loew. On the grounds of the synagogue the great rabbi and his assistants molded the golem out of clay. Rabbi Loew understood the secret of life, and from his own breath gave life to the golem. But one day the golem had a rage and destroyed everything in its way. Then the great rabbi had to destroy his own creation. The remains of the golem were said to be in the loft of the Altneuschul.

"Have you ever seen the remains?" Mikul asked.

"Nobody has. They're buried in the loft."

"I see. I wonder how often that happens."

"What?"

"How often people have to destroy what they create because their creation gets out of control."

Rivka had never thought of the story in that way. As a young child she'd been frightened and fascinated by the idea of a clay model coming to life and then going on a destructive rampage. She'd also been proud that she, Rivka Liebermann, was descended from the great and magical Rabbi Loew, who could work such miracles. When Jakob returned, she must remember to tell him about Mikul's way of seeing the story. She was sure that Jakob, who liked nothing better than finding the wisdom in common stories, would admire Mikul's interpretation.

Mikul asked about her neighbors, and she told him all about the Brandeises and how her family often ate supper with them. She told him about her grandmother and aunts who lived on the ground floor of their building, and Chavele, who had lived there before getting married.

Rivka's mother had always told her never to talk too much in the presence of a man. But here Rivka was, chattering away. She answered all Mikul's questions in great detail, simply because he appeared interested. Also, it didn't seem to matter much, at this point, if she did a few more things wrong. Look at all the rules she was already breaking.

Mikul reached into his pocket and said, "I can't take your money. I'm sure you need it."

She understood his pride was wounded. "I want you to have it," she said.

"Rivka, it's your money."

To make it easier for him, she said, "Later, after you're with your aunt and uncle, you can pay me back if you want."

He looked at the coins in his hand. "Thank you, Rivka."

"I should go back now. Soon it will be noon."

"All right."

Before leaving, she stood under the arched branches to see, one last time, the view of the city. She said a silent good-bye and then walked behind Mikul as he followed the narrow trail down the hill to the river. By now Rivka felt as familiar with this road as with some of the streets in the quarter. The Stone Bridge, distant at first, grew closer. With the sun just overhead, the statues on the bridge were brightly lit. It seemed to Rivka that in full sunlight the statues were less frightening.

As they crossed the bridge, she was startled by a cry from the other side: "Rivka! Rivka!"

It was Friedl, running toward her. "Oh, Rivka! Everyone is looking for you!"

Like a frightened animal, Rivka raised herself up on the balls of her feet. Every instinct told her to run home as fast as she could and find her mother. But first she had to know what had happened. Again Friedl said, "Oh, Rivka!"

"Tell me," she said. In her peripheral vision, she

saw Mikul take a few steps back until he was at the railing of the bridge, saving her the embarrassment of getting caught with him.

"Your father talked to my grandmother and found out you were not with me. Right away he started searching. Now everybody is searching. I've never seen him so angry. I've never seen your mother so upset."

All Rivka could do was stare.

"I'm so sorry," said Friedl. "I didn't know what to say! I couldn't lie, I just couldn't. Your father talked to Chavele, too."

Coming toward them from the other side of the bridge was Mr. Brandeis. Everyone indeed must be out looking for her. Without a glance back at Mikul, Rivka ran past Friedl and Friedl's father. She ran and ran until she was at the gates of the quarter. She ran so hard that breathing was difficult and her heart pounded violently.

At the gate, the guard said, "Are you Rivka Liebermann?" His eyebrows were raised, and she thought he had the hint of a smile on his face. She didn't answer but started running again. What a fool she had been to think she wouldn't get caught. She'd been lucky the first three times. Why, oh why, had she taken another chance?

She hoped nobody was home so she could change back into her own clothes. Facing her father dressed as a Gentile boy would make him even angrier. As she ran she took off her cap and shook her braids loose. Her hair tumbled down her back, and loose tendrils blew into her face. She stopped to catch her breath and utter a prayer. She began, "Dear God, Master of the Universe—" but could not even think of how to continue. How, then, would she find the words to give her father an explanation?

12

Rivka turned the corner of her block and saw a group of women at the foot of the stairs of her building, huddled close, talking. Among them were her mother, her grandmother, and Friedl's mother. Also there was a woman from across the street and Chavele's mother. Rivka's grandmother saw her first and gave a small shriek.

Her mother came forward to hug her. "Rivka. What have you done?"

Rivka allowed herself the comfort of sinking against her mother. Her heart pounded so hard she thought it would explode. She hated that so many people were watching her. "Mama, I'll go upstairs to change."

"We'll go together," her mother said. Rivka didn't speak as they walked up the stairs. She was too out of breath. And she was too scared. Once inside, she went into her room to change into her own clothes, and her mother followed. Rivka's hands were trembling so badly she could not fasten her bodice, and her mother had to do it for her.

Then her mother sat down on Rivka's bed and said, "It's time to tell me what has been going on."

Rivka sank onto the bed beside her mother. "The first time I was only going to leave the quarter once, to see for myself—"

"Your father took you out when you asked. That wasn't good enough?"

"I don't know why, Mama, but it wasn't. I needed time to see for myself. I thought if I could only see the hills once I'd be happy. When Papa and I went, I didn't get to see anything, not really. Then I had Mikul's oak chips, and I had to return them because he was in prison. I tried to talk to you and Papa, but you told me never to mention him again—"

Rivka's mother stared at her as her story tumbled out in this haphazard fashion. Uninterested in sorting out the details, she kept repeating, "Oh, Rivka, Rivka, what have you done?"

Not long after, Rivka and her mother were sitting at the table when the door opened and her father came in. His face was drawn tight, his motions quick and abrupt as he closed the door behind him and strode toward them without taking off his coat. Rivka, frightened, could see that he was about to explode.

"Rivka," he said, "you have deceived your parents and broken the law."

This was no small matter, Rivka knew. "I am sorry, Papa."

"When have you ever been defiant, Rivka?" Color came into her father's face, and his eyes flashed. "When have you ever disobeyed? What has gotten into you?"

She thought it better not to answer when he was in such a fury.

"Can you be my daughter?" he shouted. "Can my

daughter be so defiant? You will be fortunate—we will all be fortunate—if Oskar Kara does not call off the engagement because of what you have done."

This frightened her even more. Would Oskar indeed call off their engagement? She understood the humiliation her family would endure if he did.

Rivka felt her mother shift in her chair beside her. She sensed that her mother, too, was afraid.

He turned to her mother and said, "She is not to leave this building. For any reason."

Her father had often treated Rivka as if she was of little consequence. But he had never given orders in her presence as if she were not even there. Rivka felt humiliated, and the sensation angered her. She wanted her father to know that she was not a child. She was engaged to be married. She was almost a grown woman. True, she had disobeyed, and she was sorry for that, but her father had not listened when she had asked for his help. The problem, which he wasn't seeing, was that he, too, was at fault.

He turned to go, then stopped and looked at Rivka's mother once more. He repeated, "She is not to leave the building. For any reason." Then he left, closing the door behind him. Rivka listened to his footsteps on the stairs.

It was true that Rivka had never before been defiant. She had always been praised and loved for her goodness and compliance, and looking back, she could now see that she had been afraid of losing her parents' love. Perhaps she did not have the meek and submissive spirit her father required of her. Maybe soon he would stop loving her and would never love her again.

"Rivka," her mother said. "What is between you and this Christian boy?"

"Nothing, Mama," she said, startled. "Really. He was friendly, and I wanted to help him. He showed me beautiful places, and we talked."

"You talked? You talked about what?"

"He told me about his family, and I told him about mine. I was curious about the outside. I wanted to see it so badly. That is all, Mama. Really."

"If Oskar Kara calls off the engagement, nobody will believe that nothing happened between you and that boy."

Rivka thought it was wrong for her mother to refer to Mikul as a boy. He was a grown man, and a hardworking one at that. What Rivka wanted just then was to speak to Oskar. This sudden desire startled her, but she felt that if she could explain everything to him, he would understand. After all, everyone said he was a good man. But she didn't ask her mother's permission to call for Oskar. Her mother would say she couldn't talk to Oskar without first asking her father, and he would most certainly forbid it.

Rivka heard someone on the landing. She thought perhaps her father had returned until she heard three light taps on the door. She jumped up and went to open it. It was Friedl, who whispered, "I have to tell you something."

"Stay inside, Rivka," her mother said. "You heard your father."

Friedl said, "I want to make sure Rivka is all right, Mrs. Liebermann."

"She's all right," said Rivka's mother wearily, getting up and going into her bedroom.

Friedl stepped inside, and Rivka closed the door. Friedl whispered, "I tried not to tell, but once your father started asking me questions, what could I do? Chavele answered his questions, too. I wasn't the only one—"

"It doesn't matter," Rivka said.

Very quietly Friedl whispered, "That man talked to me."

"What man?" Rivka whispered. "Mikul?"

"After you ran away, he followed us home."

"What did he say?"

"He is afraid for you. He wants to talk to you." Friedl's eyes were shining. Rivka had the feeling she enjoyed being part of this adventure. Nothing like this had ever happened before.

"I can't talk to him again. I'm already in enough trouble."

"He said he'll come to the main gate tonight at eleven. He'll come for the next three nights until you meet him. He just wants to talk to you. He wants to make sure you're all right. Rivka, are you in love with him?"

"Don't be ridiculous. No." Rivka glanced toward her parents' bedroom to make sure her mother was out of earshot and then said, "Friedl, you must do something for me. Go get Oskar Kara, please. I want to talk to him."

"Why?"

"I just do."

"But why?" Friedl insisted.

Rivka wanted to find out for herself how Oskar would react to her story. If he responded as she hoped, the trouble might straighten itself out.

Just then her mother came back into the room, and Rivka couldn't say any more. As Friedl said good-bye, Rivka again had the feeling she was enjoying all the excitement. She hoped Friedl would indeed go look for Oskar.

Rivka and her mother sat back down at the table. Her mother began to lecture her. "Rivka, you must promise never to leave again. What if you get caught out there? These are serious matters, very serious."

"I won't leave again, Mama, I promise." As Rivka said these words she realized what they meant: she'd never again see the wide-open sky stretching forever or smell the mossy, woodsy scent of the forest. She felt a deep sadness and a new fear—could she really keep such a promise?

Less than an hour later, there was a knock at the door, and Rivka answered it. It was Oskar Kara, who said, "You want to talk to me?"

Rivka tried to read his expression but couldn't. He studied her steadily, curiously.

Rivka's mother came up behind her and said, "Rivka, what is this about?"

"Mama, I need to talk to him. There is something I want to tell him."

Rivka could feel her mother's tension. "There is nothing you have to tell him." She looked pleadingly at Oskar. "I don't know what this is about."

"I would like to hear what Rivka has to say."

Rivka was afraid to search Oskar's face for clues as to how he felt, and she could read nothing in his voice. For all she could tell, he might be angry. Maybe Papa was right, and Oskar would call off the engagement and nobody else would ever want to marry her. She'd have to live at home with her parents for the rest of her life.

Oskar said, "Come outside, Rivka."

Rivka's mother wouldn't contradict Oskar any more than she would her own husband, even on a matter of propriety such as this.

Oskar took a step back and gestured for Rivka to come out onto the landing. Rivka stepped outside and closed the door. She wondered if her mother would try to eavesdrop on their conversation.

"Let's go down here," she suggested. If they went down the six steps to the next landing, her mother wouldn't be able to hear them even if she opened the door a crack. Oskar let her go first and then followed. Rivka reached the landing and turned around but had difficulty looking directly at him.

Never before had she talked to Oskar alone. Some

girls, by chance or necessity, did talk alone to their betrothed, but the custom was to wait until after the wedding. She wondered what Oskar thought of this spontaneous meeting that she had initiated.

"I just want to explain," she began timidly. "I want to tell you what happened, because my papa said you may be angry. I want to explain why I went out." She hesitated, trying to get a sense of his reaction.

"Go on."

"Jakob told me stories about what the outside was like, about the forests and fields. My papa took me out once, but it wasn't enough. I needed more time there. I needed to see things for myself."

He rubbed his chin, considering. It occurred to her that this was the wrong thing to say. Maybe Oskar was imagining his wife leaving the quarter whenever the mood struck her. She said, "I won't do it again."

"Did you really dress as a Gentile boy?"

"Mama told me how badly people out there treat Jews, so I didn't want anyone to know I was Jewish."

"People actually thought you were a boy?"

"One girl selling eggs called me 'sir.'"

Oskar fingered the railing thoughtfully. "What did you do out there?"

Rivka told him all about her adventures. She told him how she had harvested potatoes and how she had to go a second time so she could see the forest. Then she told him about Mikul and how kind he had been to her, and how he was arrested and put into prison.

Suddenly the door upstairs opened, and her mother stepped out. "We're down here," Oskar called up to her. "We'll be a few more minutes."

Rivka's mother stood for a moment staring at them, then returned inside, softly closing the door.

Rivka said, "I don't know what she thinks I'm going to do. I guess she doesn't trust me anymore." She sighed and continued with her story. She told Oskar about Mikul's oak chips and going out a third time to redeem them. She told him about how Mikul came to the marketplace and invited her out once more. Here, she knew, she was on dangerous ground. The only reason she went this last time was to see the beautiful view that Mikul had promised to show her.

She stole a glance at Oskar, but he didn't seem disturbed. She had the feeling he was just trying to understand. Then he said, "Tell me about Mikul's debt. Why is he in trouble?"

So she explained, emphasizing that what Mikul really wanted was to pay his debt so he could join his family in Germany. As she told the story, she became aware of how intently Oskar was listening to everything she had to say. Unlike her father, he wanted to know what happened.

When she finished, he said, "Let's sit down." Now she was certain he wasn't angry. They sat on the landing dangling their feet in exactly the same way Rivka sat with Friedl and Chavele. How odd to see Oskar sitting that way, like a young boy, like someone who could be her friend.

He said, "I don't understand why your father is so angry about this. Maybe he doesn't realize how innocent it all is."

"Innocent?" she said. She didn't think she was innocent. After all, she had left the quarter in disguise to visit a young man, and she had deceived her parents.

"Well, not exactly innocent," he said. "But it isn't as bad as it sounded at first. Unless there is something you're not telling."

"I've told you everything. I promised my mama I'd never go out again."

"But you will want to go out again, won't you?" A light came into his face, and she sensed he was more amused than angry. She could hardly believe his reaction. What man wanted a willful wife? She gripped the iron railing in front of her and leaned her forehead against the cold metal. She could tell him the truth, or she could lie. It seemed the sensible and safe thing to do was lie. But something that she didn't understand made her say, "I guess I will want to go again."

"Why wasn't it enough to go with your father?"

"He walked too fast. He didn't allow me to see anything, not really."

Oskar looked down at the alley. Rivka studied his profile, knowing she shouldn't be staring. She thought there was a gentleness to his expression. Then he said, "I remember the first time I went out. I was ten. I didn't understand why we had to live in here, surrounded by walls."

"Do you understand now?"

"Sometimes. But other times the walls don't make sense."

"There have been walls forever," she said. "Or almost forever."

"Some people," he said, looking at her, "Christians and Jews, mostly younger people, don't think there should be walls."

Rivka considered this. She could not imagine the Jewish quarter without walls and gates. Mikul had no hostility toward Jews, and there must be other Christians like him, but still she couldn't imagine a world without walls separating different people.

"Rivka," Oskar said, "if I don't walk fast, and if you have time to see things, would you be content to go with me? After we're married, of course."

His words so surprised her that it took her a moment to understand what he was saying. She felt, just then, that there was something familiar about him. He had a way of tilting his head slightly as if listening intently, like Jakob. Oskar said, "Unless you don't want to go with me. Maybe it's only an exciting adventure when you're with strange Christian men."

"No." Then she saw from the light in his eyes that he was teasing. She smiled at him, and he smiled back. Perhaps Oskar, too, felt frightened and shy. Suddenly the thought came to her that the man sitting beside her would someday be her husband. Her stomach fluttered nervously. At such a time she expected the ache to come into her stomach, but it didn't. She felt jittery, and that was all.

"Good. Then we can go together. Now, Rivka, it's important that you're not hiding any more surprises. Your father can be very rigid about these things. Is there anything else I should know?"

She thought this over. "Mikul sent me a message, through Friedl, that he wants to talk to me. I told Friedl I can't, I'm already in enough trouble."

"Please don't talk to him, Rivka. Your father will never understand."

"I know." She lifted her chin boldly, looking at him as she had looked at people when she'd been dressed as a boy. He didn't seem to mind. She said, "I promise I won't talk to him."

"But will you want to? Will you have a burning desire to talk to him, do you think?"

"No. I just wish he could pay his debt and go to his family in Germany."

Oskar studied her for such a long time that she looked down at her hands. At last he stood up and said, "You'd better go in. Your mother doesn't like this one bit."

He offered his hand and helped her up. She smiled at him gratefully. She wanted to say thank you. Instead, overcome with shyness, she walked up the stairs and opened the door. She looked back to find him watching her.

13

That evening at supper Rivka's father was quiet. He seemed calm, which surprised her. She imagined he would still be angry. After a long silence, he startled her by looking at her and saying, "Oskar Kara put a request before the Jewish council this afternoon." Rivka set down her fork and waited. "He has requested charity funds to pay the debt of that Christian man, your friend."

"Will they do it?" she asked.

"I doubt it."

Rivka realized at once that Oskar had done this because she had told him she wished Mikul could pay his debts and go to his family in Germany. She thought this was Oskar's way of saying that he believed her and trusted her. For months, her mother had been saying he was a good man. Now, finally, Rivka believed it herself. What she felt just then was a warm contentment.

The following day, a letter came from Jakob. He reported that he had arrived safely, he was settled into his new room, he liked the young men he was living with, and he was eager to begin his studies. Nathan asked to read the letter so many times that by the time Rivka's father came home, it was smeared and tattered. The following day they would send a letter back to him. Each member of the family would write something. Rivka suspected that her portion of the letter would be the longest.

That evening, Rivka's family had just sat down to dinner when a knock came at the door. Rivka's father got up to answer it. It was not unusual for him to be summoned in the evenings to someone's sickbed. To Rivka's surprise, it was Oskar. She sat up straighter in her chair, listening. Oskar said, "I'm sorry to bother you, Dr. Liebermann. May I speak to Rivka for a moment? I won't be long."

Rivka looked at her mother, who whispered, "Stay inside."

Rivka stood up and went to the door. Oskar, who evidently had not heard Rivka's mother's command, said, "We'll be out on the landing."

Her parents glanced at each other. Oskar, taking their silence for assent, stepped outside and beckoned for Rivka to follow. Then her father said, "Leave the door open, please."

Rivka and Oskar stood by the railing, within sight but out of hearing of her parents. Oskar whispered, "I asked the council to help your friend. They refused."

She smiled at him. The evening air was cool, and the breeze felt good on her forehead. She felt calm and serene. She put her hands on the railing and said, "Thank you for trying."

He said, "I can give him enough money to help him get to Germany."

She wanted to say, You would really do that? but found she couldn't speak at all. Jakob, too, would have wanted to help Mikul. She managed to say, "But Mikul's proud."

"I can imagine. I'd have a hard time taking the money, too. I'll tell him it's a loan. He can pay me back after he finds work in Germany. But, Rivka, remember that we can't help everyone out there who needs it. We can't even help everyone in here who needs it. I'm helping Mikul because you said he was kind to you. And to tell you the truth, I'll feel better when he's far away."

She felt uneasy. Had she already given her future husband reason to distrust her? "I'm sorry."

He shrugged. "You did what you had to do. Now we just have to get the money to Mikul. Do you know where I can find him?"

"He told Friedl he'd come to the main gate at eleven o'clock hoping to talk to me."

"All right. You'd better go back inside. I don't think your father likes us out here like this."

His eyes were bright, as if he were about to smile. She had the feeling he was faintly amused. The possibility of being amused instead of frightened by her father made Rivka feel lighter and happier. She smiled and said, "I'm sure he doesn't like this at all."

They exchanged good-byes, and then she went back in and closed the door behind her.

Her father waited until she returned to her seat, then said, "What did Oskar want?" She noticed that he asked the question calmly, perhaps even respectfully, in a tone he might use in talking to her mother. Was this because he respected and trusted Oskar? Or was it because he realized he might have judged her too harshly?

"He wants to help Mikul. That's all."

"Who is Mikul?" asked Nathan.

"Never mind," said Rivka's mother.

At bedtime that night, Rivka went into her room and opened the door leading to the roof so she could feel the fresh, cool air on her face. From the street came the cry of the night watchman: "Nine o'clock, and all is well." In two hours, Mikul and Oskar would meet at the main gate. The gates would be locked, but they'd be able to talk through the bars. She was confident that Oskar could convince Mikul to take the money.

She had so envied Jakob setting off to see the outside world of charming villages and forests stretching on forever. Now she, too, had seen the forests and the world beyond the walls. She had even seen Mikul's room and worked in the fields. She was, quite possibly, the only girl in the entire quarter who had ever befriended a Christian man. What was more, she understood more than her father—she understood that helping Mikul had been the right thing to do.

Yes, all was well. She heard a thump on the wall separating her brothers' room from her own, and she knew they were wrestling in bed instead of sleeping. In the lamplight of the neighboring building, she saw a white cat move on the stairs. The shadow cast by the ladder's metal rungs reminded her of the iron grill of the quarter gates. From below she heard the sound of her neighbors' voices, friendly and soothing, bidding each other good-night.

Afterword

Rivka's adventures in the outside world heralded great changes to come. Two years after Rivka and Oskar were married, the new emperor passed the Toleration Edict giving Jews new freedoms. The Toleration Edict marked the beginning of the emancipation of the Jews—but it was just the beginning. Change came slowly. First curfews were abolished, then Jews were permitted to attend Prague's university. In time they could move freely around Prague and were able to join the larger culture. The Jews, who so valued books and learning, would contribute much to Prague's cultural and literary greatness. Rivka's grandchildren would enjoy the rights of full citizenship and would only know about locked gates and guards from history books and handed-down stories. After 1848 the Jews of Prague would be fully emancipated, and the close restrictions of ghetto life, which had continued unbroken for hundreds of years, would come to an end.

Acknowledgments

Special thanks to Dr. Dean Bell at the Spertus Institute of Jewish Studies; Professor Wilma Iggers at Canisius College, an expert in Bohemian Jewish history; Daniel Stuhlman at the Hebrew Theological College; Rabbi Greg Wolfe with the Congregation Bet–Havarim; Laura Tillotson, a gifted editor; Janet Rosen with Sheree Bykofsky Associates; and Betsy Wattenberg, who has long been my best critic.